Love in Small Places

Judy Best

Copyright © 2024 by Judy Best

All rights reserved.

The content contained within this book may not be reproduced, duplicated, or transmitted without direct written permission from the author or the publisher.

Under no circumstances will any blame or legal responsibility be held against the publisher or author for any damages, reparation, or monetary loss due to the information contained within this book, either directly or indirectly.

Legal Notice: This book is copyright-protected. It is only for personal use. You cannot amend, distribute, sell, use, quote, or paraphrase any part of this book's content without the author's or publisher's consent.

Disclaimer Notice: Please note the information contained within this document is for educational and entertainment purposes only. All efforts have been executed to present accurate, up-to-date, reliable, and complete information. No warranties of any kind are declared or implied. Readers acknowledge that the author is not engaged in the rendering of legal, financial, medical, or professional advice. The content of this book has been derived from various sources. Please consult a licensed professional before attempting any techniques outlined in this book.

By reading this document, the reader agrees that the author is under no circumstances responsible for any direct or indirect losses incurred as a result of using the information contained within it, including, but not limited to, errors, omissions, or inaccuracies.

This is a work of fiction. Unless otherwise indicated, all the names, characters, businesses, places, events and incidents in this book are either the product of the author's imagination or used in a fictitious manner. Any resemblance to actual persons, living or dead, or actual events is purely coincidental.

Contents

1. The Return of Luke Hunter — 1
2. Old Flames, New Problems — 11
3. Hidden Truths and New Deals — 21
4. Lingering Questions — 29
5. A Walk Down Memory Lane — 35
6. Secrets, Schemes and Spilled Tea — 43
7. Digging for the Truth — 53
8. A Little Help From My Friends — 65
9. Family Ties and Seeking Truth — 75
10. Secrets & Strategies — 85
11. Showdowns & Unexpected Alliances — 95
12. Fishing for Clues — 109
13. Disappearances & Hidden Agendas — 127
14. Suspicious Minds — 137
15. The Net Tightens — 159
16. Desperate Moves — 169

17.	Founder's Day Preparations	179
18.	Founder's Day Eve	189
19.	Founder's Day Event Begins	201
20.	Confrontation on Founder's Day	211
21.	A Surprise and A Proposal	219
22.	A Carter's Creek Wedding	227
23.	Getting on With Forever!	237
About the Author		244

Chapter One
The Return of Luke Hunter

The morning light filtered through the windows of Emma Thompson's office as she signed another permit, her third today. Being the mayor of Carter's Creek was never on her life plan, but here she was—running the town she grew up in, the daughter of the pastor, living in a place where everyone knew her name.

The town square, with its cobblestone paths and colorful planters, was buzzing outside her window. Right across the street was the Southern Roots Tavern. Even after all these years, Emma couldn't walk by without glancing at the corner booth where she and Luke Hunter spent countless summers laughing and dreaming, before life carried him off like the wind.

Rumor had it he was back in town. Probably passing through on his way to some new adventure. Luke was never the stay-in-one-place type, and while Carter's Creek had its charm, it wasn't built for the likes of him—dreamers who always had one foot out the door. Not like her.

"*Mayor Thompson!*" The sound of her secretary's voice cut through her thoughts. "*Luke Hunter is here to see you.*"

Her heart skipped a beat. Luke Hunter, here? Now? She hadn't seen him in what... ten years?

She straightened her jacket, trying to calm the wave of emotions sweeping over her. This wasn't the carefree girl of summers past; this was the mayor, a woman with responsibilities, and there was no place for old flings and wild memories in her office.

The door opened, and there he was. Taller than she remembered, his sandy hair sun-kissed, his smile the same crooked grin that had won her over at fifteen. He looked like he hadn't changed at all, except for the worn boots and the weathered hands of a man who'd been places. She could smell the road on him, that scent of freedom and distance she had long envied but never pursued.

Luke's gaze lingered on Emma longer than he'd meant to. She wasn't the girl he'd left behind all those years ago, yet something about her was just the same. Her honey-blonde hair was shorter now, cut in soft waves that framed her face. There was an air of authority in the way she held herself—shoulders squared, back straight. She wore a tailored blazer, something professional, but Luke noticed the hint of a floral dress peeking from beneath, a whisper of the carefree girl she used to be.

Her eyes, though—they hadn't changed. Still that deep green that could pierce right through him, though now there was something guarded in them, something that hadn't been there before. She was more put together, more polished, but underneath it all, he could still see the Emma who used to laugh with him by the creek, barefoot and wild, without a care in the world.

For a moment, he almost forgot why he'd come back.

"*Emma,*" he said softly, his voice smooth but carrying a weight she hadn't expected. "*It's been a while.*"

She folded her arms, trying to keep her cool, but she could already feel her resolve weakening. "*Luke Hunter, the town's wandering son. What brings you back this time?*"

He chuckled, that same low rumble that used to make her heart race. "*Got word the old gazebo was falling apart. Figured it could use some fixing.*"

Emma arched an eyebrow, surprised but suspicious. The gazebo was a town treasure, sure, but was that really why he was back?

"*So, you're here to fix the gazebo?*" she asked, her tone light but with an edge of disbelief. "*Not exactly the big city, is it?*"

He shrugged, leaning casually against her desk like he owned the place. "*Maybe it's time I slowed down. Or maybe Carter's Creek has a few things worth sticking around for.*"

There was that grin again, and for the briefest moment, it was just them, back behind the tavern, stealing kisses while the whole world kept turning. But Emma snapped back. She wasn't that girl anymore, and she couldn't afford to be.

"*Well,*" she said, trying to sound businesslike, "*if you're planning on fixing anything, you'll have to go through me. I'm the mayor now, remember?*"

Luke straightened, his gaze locking onto hers. "*Trust me, Emma. I won't be stepping on your toes... unless you want me to.*"

Her cheeks flushed, but she kept her chin high. Whatever Luke Hunter was up to, she wasn't going to fall for it. Not again.

***

Emma blinked, trying to make sense of the figure standing in her office doorway, hands shoved casually in his pockets, a smirk playing at his lips. Luke Hunter. The very name sent a rush of memories tumbling back, none of which she had invited. Yet here he was, standing just as effortlessly as he had all those years ago, like he'd simply walked out for milk and decided to drop back in ten years later.

"So, the Founder's Day Festival," Emma managed, clearing her throat and folding her arms in a show of control she didn't quite feel. "You're saying you're staying for that?"

Luke's grin only widened. "Seems like the town could use an extra pair of hands. Got some free time, and I figure I owe the old place a little love."

Emma gave a quick, noncommittal nod, though her mind spun. Founder's Day wasn't just some small-town event—it was practically the heartbeat of Carter's Creek, and a battlefield for the stubborn wills of their fathers. Tom Hunter, Luke's dad, always saw the town's future in grit and growth, pushing for practical solutions, while her father, Pastor Thompson, saw it as a celebration of tradition and unity, a reason for the community to come together. As mayor, she had spent years navigating between them, silently striking compromises, mediating their fiery debates, keeping the peace.

And now, with Luke back, it felt like those old rivalries were destined to flare up once more. Except now, he was stepping in just as casually as he'd walked away all those years ago, leaving her to carry the weight of both family legacies, both feuds.

Her gaze lingered on his face, the years fading momentarily as she remembered that summer night, the festival lights casting colors over the sky. She could still feel the rush of their shared secrets, the thrill of breaking away from the crowd, sneaking behind the old oak tree as fireworks popped in the distance. They were fifteen then, their heads full of dreams and hearts brimming with the innocent wonder of first love. She remembered the way he'd looked at her, his eyes reflecting the fireworks, his hand finding hers with a hesitant grip that spoke of nerves and excitement. His lips had met hers, soft and warm, making her believe, if only for that night, that they were something unbreakable.

But then he'd left, gone without a backward glance, and she'd been left wondering what that kiss had meant to him. To her, it had been everything.

She squared her shoulders, pushing the memory aside, determined to keep her focus on the present. "Fine," she said, her tone brisk. "But let's be clear—I'm in charge here. You'll report to me."

Luke raised his hands in a mock gesture of surrender, his smirk unfazed. "Whatever you say, boss," he replied, his voice tinged with humor.

Emma raised an eyebrow, ignoring the familiar flutter that his teasing tone still managed to stir. "I'm serious, Luke. The festival is about the town, and I won't have any of your 'free spirit' tendencies ruining the schedule."

Luke chuckled, leaning against the doorframe with that easy charm that used to drive her crazy. "Relax, Mayor Thompson. I'm here to work. Besides, if memory serves, I've always been good at following your lead."

Emma felt her face heat, and she quickly looked down at the papers on her desk. "Just remember who's in charge," she muttered, more to herself than to him.

"Understood," he said, his voice softening just slightly. "I'll do my best to keep up."

Emma glanced up, their eyes meeting in a moment that felt both nostalgic and completely unsettling. She could feel the unspoken words hovering between them, the weight of the past pressing into the present, but she refused to let it sway her. Not this time.

"Good," she said, managing a steady nod. "We'll start with the gazebo repairs tomorrow morning. I'll meet you at Town Square at eight."

"Eight it is," he replied, his gaze lingering on her for just a second too long before he turned to go.

As he stepped out, Emma let out a breath she hadn't realized she was holding. She watched his retreating figure and felt, not for the first time, the familiar ache of what might have been. But now, she was determined to keep her feet firmly planted in the present. After all, she had a town to run—and a festival to make perfect.

***

Later that afternoon, Emma sat on a park bench in the town square, her clipboard balanced on her lap as she scanned the plans for Founder's Day. She tried to concentrate, but the steady rhythm of hammering from the gazebo kept dragging her back to memories she wasn't entirely ready to revisit. Every swing of the hammer seemed to echo with reminders—the quiet moments when Luke's hand would brush hers, the thrill of their first kiss under the moonlight, the way she had once believed that he'd always be there.

She shook her head, trying to clear it. They'd been kids, and those moments were better left in the past. Yet, here he was, as real as the gazebo he was rebuilding, and those feelings she thought she'd buried didn't seem as distant as she'd hoped.

Her phone buzzed, jolting her from her thoughts. She glanced down to see a message from her best friend, Hannah.

THE RETURN OF LUKE HUNTER

I saw Luke's back. Guess that's going to make things... interesting?

Emma rolled her eyes, typing a quick reply. *Not interesting. He's just here to fix the gazebo.*

Oh, sure. Just to fix the gazebo, Hannah replied, followed by an exaggerated eye-roll emoji. *Bet the gossips are losing their minds.*

Emma sighed, glancing up from her phone toward the Dew Drop Inn across the street. Sure enough, Ms. Beatrice, the town's resident expert on everyone else's business, was positioned by the window, peering over her coffee cup with a level of scrutiny that could have uncovered government secrets. She was leaning close to her friend, Mabel, her gaze flitting from Emma to the gazebo and back again. The animated whispering left no doubt—they'd noticed Luke and Emma working together.

Emma could practically feel the gossip ripple outward, like a stone dropped into a pond. By evening, half the town would know that Luke Hunter was back in Carter's Creek, and that he was working with her. Just what she needed.

Her phone buzzed again. *So, spill. You and Luke together all day... any sparks?*

She scowled, shooting a quick reply. *Hannah, we're just working.*

But even as she typed the words, she couldn't ignore the tiny pang in her chest. Because no matter how much she told herself that Luke's return was purely business, she couldn't shake the memories his presence stirred. She looked up again, and her gaze landed on him just as he paused his work, wiping the sweat from his forehead. For a second, their eyes met across the square, and Luke offered a quick smile—a familiar one that seemed to say, *Remember when?*

Emma quickly looked away, pressing her lips together and hoping she could convince herself as much as Hannah that it was all strictly professional.

Her phone buzzed one last time. *If it's just business, you've got nothing to worry about... but if you ask me, a little spark never hurt anyone.*

Emma sighed, tossing her phone back into her bag. She needed to keep her mind on the festival. She couldn't afford to let Luke—or the gossips—distract her from the job she'd worked so hard to do.

But as she glanced back at the gazebo, she couldn't shake the feeling that maybe, just maybe, things were about to get a lot more complicated.

***

By the time Emma made her way to the gazebo, Luke was already wiping his hands on a rag. The structure looked no better, still as rundown as before, but he'd clearly been hard at work loosening broken boards.

"You gonna stand there all day, or did you come to lend a hand?" Luke teased, tossing the rag into his tool bag.

Emma sighed. "I'm here to see how much progress you've made."

"Still the same Emma. Always wanting things just right." He stepped closer, his eyes glinting with amusement. "It's a work in progress."

"So you've said," she shot back. "It's not like we have all the time in the world. Founder's Day is only a month away."

Luke's smile faded, and for a second, she saw something else in his eyes. Something that made her heart skip.

"I know," he said quietly. "I won't let you down this time."

Emma blinked, caught off guard by the weight of his words. This time? What did he mean by that? But before she could ask, a familiar voice rang out behind them.

"Luke Hunter, as I live and breathe!"

THE RETURN OF LUKE HUNTER

Both Emma and Luke turned to see Tom Hunter walking up, his broad grin aimed at his son. Luke stiffened, his hands dropping to his sides. The tension between them was thick enough to slice with a knife.

"Dad," Luke muttered, his tone clipped. "Didn't expect you here."

"Didn't expect you back in town, either," Tom said, his voice casual but with an undercurrent of something darker. "Figured you'd be halfway across the world by now."

Emma glanced between them, feeling the air shift. Everyone in town knew the relationship between Luke and his dad had been strained for years, ever since Luke left Carter's Creek without looking back. Tom had always been a stickler for staying local, putting down roots. Luke? Not so much.

"Guess I'm sticking around for a bit," Luke said, his tone light but his jaw clenched.

"Well, don't go making promises you can't keep," Tom replied, his words barbed.

The tension crackled between father and son, and Emma could feel the weight of old wounds lingering in the air. It was a small-town thing. Everyone knew everyone's business, and no one ever forgot.

Emma cleared her throat, stepping forward. "The gazebo needs to be finished for the festival, Tom. Luke's been a big help so far."

Tom gave a slow nod, but his eyes never left his son. "Just make sure you're here when it counts."

Luke's fists clenched at his sides, but he said nothing. As Tom walked away, Luke muttered under his breath, "Same old dad."

Emma wanted to say something—anything—but she couldn't find the words. Instead, she found herself wondering if Luke really would stick around. Or if, just like always, he'd be gone before the dust settled.

Chapter Two
Old Flames, New Problems

THE NEXT MORNING, EMMA sat across from her best friend, Hannah, in their usual cozy corner booth at the Dew Drop Inn. The sunlight streamed through the window, illuminating dust motes that drifted lazily in the air, as if even they were in no rush. Emma absently stirred her coffee, staring at the swirling patterns but not really seeing them. She was trying to focus on anything but Luke, but the memories from the night before played in her mind on a loop.

"You've been quiet all morning," Hannah said, her tone light but knowing as she raised an eyebrow. "This wouldn't have anything to do with a certain someone being back in town, would it?"

Emma rolled her eyes, though she couldn't quite hide the smile tugging at the corners of her lips. "I knew you were going to say something."

"Well, it's not like Luke Hunter can just stroll back into Carter's Creek without turning a few heads. I saw the way you looked at him yesterday," Hannah said, leaning forward with a smirk that only deepened Emma's blush.

Emma sighed, forcing herself to shake her head, as if that would dismiss the lingering feelings she'd been trying to forget for years. "It's not like that anymore, Han. That was a long time ago."

Hannah's eyes sparkled with that mischievous glint Emma knew all too well. "So, you don't get even a little heart flutter when you see him? Don't tell me you've forgotten about all those summers you spent together. Or how you once told me—what was it again? Oh, right, that Luke Hunter was 'the one.'"

Emma shifted uncomfortably, a flicker of nostalgia creeping up despite her best efforts to keep it at bay. "People change, Hannah. I've changed. He's changed. Luke's... different now. He's not exactly the stay-in-one-place type."

"And you're still the one making excuses," Hannah teased, taking a sip of her coffee. "You can deny it all you want, but there's still something between you two. It's practically written on your face."

Emma tried to give her a warning look, but her thoughts betrayed her, drifting back to that summer evening under the old oak tree near the edge of town. The way they'd stolen away from everyone, his hand warm and steady as it lingered over hers, how he'd pulled her close, his eyes meeting hers with a promise she'd never forgotten. His lips had brushed hers so softly, so carefully, that it felt like the whole world had stopped spinning just for them.

"It's just... it's complicated," Emma finally muttered, almost as if trying to convince herself.

"Love usually is," Hannah said, with a hint of tenderness breaking through her teasing tone. "But complicated doesn't mean impossible. Sometimes it just takes a little bravery to see if the past still fits into the present."

Emma looked down at her coffee, unwilling to admit that Hannah might be right, that she might not be as over Luke Hunter as she tried to appear. Because somewhere, deep down, the thought of what they'd had was as vivid as ever—just waiting for a reason to come alive again.

***

Across town, Luke sat with his best friend, Tommy, in the back room of Walker's Hardware & Supply, the hardware store Tommy's family has owned forever, but which Tommy now runs on his own. The familiar scent of sawdust and fresh lumber filled the air, grounding him in a place that hadn't changed much since they were kids. Tommy passed him a cold soda, leaning against the workbench with a knowing smirk.

"So," Tommy began, drawing out the word, "back in town for two days, and you're already fixing gazebos and, what's this I hear—working with Emma Thompson?"

Luke rolled his eyes, popping the soda open. "You know, for a town this small, news sure travels fast."

"Fast?" Tommy snorted. "Gossip here is basically teleportation. Word is Ms. Beatrice practically ran out of the Dew Drop Inn yesterday after seeing you and Emma together. I heard she even dropped her coffee."

Luke shook his head, trying to fight off the smile that tugged at his lips. "It's nothing, Tommy. Just helping with the festival. That's all."

Tommy raised an eyebrow, giving Luke a skeptical look. "Come on, man. You and Emma—it was never just 'nothing.' Everyone knew you two were going somewhere special... before you left, anyway."

Luke's smile faded slightly, and he took a sip of soda, his gaze drifting to the open door and the sunlight streaming through. "That was a long time ago, Tommy. She's got her own life now, and I've got mine."

Tommy crossed his arms, leaning in closer. "Maybe, but that doesn't mean either of you has really moved on. Look, it was obvious to everyone—you two were like fire and gasoline. And hey, you're back now. Why not see if there's still a spark?"

Luke chuckled, though the idea unsettled him more than he'd like to admit. "Could've. Should've. But I didn't," he muttered, his tone carrying a hint of regret.

"Doesn't mean you can't now," Tommy said, shrugging in that easy-going way of his. "Maybe it's time to stop looking at what went wrong and start thinking about what could go right."

Luke sat back, rolling the soda can between his hands, his mind swirling with memories of the days he and Emma would spend under the summer sun, dreaming of a life that felt within arm's reach. "Sometimes it feels like... like being back here just reopens all the old wounds, you know?"

Tommy gave him a serious nod. "Maybe it's the universe giving you a second chance, man. Doesn't happen often. Not to mention, from what I hear, Emma's been just as distracted."

Luke looked up, trying to keep his voice casual. "You think?"

Tommy smirked, his eyes glinting. "Saw her yesterday, and trust me, she still looks at you the same way she used to. Even if she doesn't want to admit it."

Luke didn't respond, lost in thought. Part of him wanted to believe that things could be different this time, that the love they'd shared hadn't faded as much as he thought. But the other part knew the risks of reopening that door. Still, he couldn't deny that being back, seeing her again, made him wonder if the story of Emma and him was really over—or if, just maybe, it was waiting for a new beginning.

***

The Town Hall meeting room buzzed with chatter as committee members settled into their seats. Emma sat at the head of the long, polished table, her fingers tapping on the stack of paperwork she'd prepared, while across the room, Luke leaned against the back wall, arms crossed, scanning the gathering with a thoughtful expression. His father, Tom Hunter, was already grumbling as he thumbed through the budget sheets in front of him.

"We can't keep increasing the budget for a bunch of decorations that'll be gone in a week," Tom said, his voice gruff with conviction. "We need to focus on what's lasting—like fixing the gazebo and keeping things practical."

Across the table, Pastor Daniel Thompson folded his arms, arching an eyebrow in Tom's direction. "This festival is about celebrating our history, Tom. The decorations are a part of that legacy. For decades, people have come to see Carter's Creek dressed up for Founder's Day. They expect the town to look its best."

Emma sighed, glancing over the room as murmurs of agreement rippled through some of the committee members. She cast a quick look at Luke, who returned it with a small, knowing smile, one that mirrored the mix of exasperation and amusement they'd shared many times growing up. It was as if nothing had changed—Tom and Pastor Thompson were at it again, and once more, Emma found herself in the middle of their age-old debates.

But her father and Tom weren't the only ones with opinions. To Emma's right, Ms. Beatrice leaned over to whisper with a few other committee members, their heads close together as they cast subtle glances between Emma and Luke, clearly intrigued by the fact that the two of them were working together on the festival.

"Maybe we should all focus on the bigger picture here," Emma said, raising her voice enough to quiet the murmuring. "The gazebo will be ready in time, and we'll make sure the festival reflects both our town's history and its future. We can strike a balance."

Pastor Thompson nodded approvingly, but Tom still looked unconvinced, his lips pressed into a thin line. "As long as you're not wasting money on unnecessary frills, I'm fine with it."

Ms. Beatrice cleared her throat, and Emma braced herself. "Well, decorations or not, I'm more interested in how lovely it is to see certain... people back in town. I heard the festival team will be working very closely together this year," she said, her eyes flicking from Emma to Luke with a smile that left little room for misinterpretation.

A few chuckles broke out, and Emma felt her cheeks heat, but she kept her tone steady. "Yes, well, that's part of why Luke's here—to lend his skills on the gazebo." She tried to ignore Ms. Beatrice's amused look as she continued, "Now, let's refocus. I think we can work out a compromise on the budget if we—"

But her voice trailed off as she noticed Luke stifling a grin from his spot at the back of the room. Their eyes met again, and he gave her a small, reassuring nod, as if to say, *You've got this.* She allowed herself a faint smile in return, feeling a sense of support that, for some reason, made her task a little easier.

As the meeting continued, Emma realized with a hint of resignation that it was going to be a long festival season. Between managing budgets, mediating old feuds, and keeping the town gossip at bay, her plate was more than full. But glancing back at Luke, she couldn't shake the feeling that having him around—no matter how complicated it made things—was more of a help than a hindrance.

***

Luke wiped his brow, the late afternoon sun casting long shadows as he tightened a loose board on the gazebo floor. Every few minutes, he couldn't resist a quick glance at the second-floor window just across the square, the one he knew belonged to Emma's office. He wondered if she'd noticed him yet, though a part of him hoped she hadn't, feeling a bit like a lovestruck teenager instead of the man who'd come back to town to make things right.

Inside her office, Emma tried for the third time to refocus on the document in front of her, but the rhythmic sound of a hammer outside pulled her mind back to him. She looked out the window, and there he was, as ruggedly handsome as she remembered, arms flexing with every swing of the hammer. She exhaled and glanced away, her heart doing that familiar skip it used to do years ago.

As she finally wrapped up her day, Emma gathered her things and strolled down the stairs, telling herself she wouldn't glance his way. But as she stepped out into the evening air, Luke looked up, catching her eye. He had been loading his tools into the back of his truck, but now he walked over, casually falling into step beside her as she made her way down the sidewalk.

"Nice evening for a walk," he said, breaking the silence between them with a slow, easy grin.

Emma couldn't help but smile back, her pulse quickening. "It is... and nice work on the gazebo. Looks like it's shaping up pretty well."

"Well," he said, glancing at her with a look that lingered just a bit too long, "I do my best work when there's good reason to stay focused."

They walked in silence for a moment, the air thick with unspoken words, before she nodded, wishing him a good evening and forcing herself to turn down her street. But as she walked away, she couldn't resist one last look back, catching him watching her too, the hint of a smile still on his face.

***

Later that evening, the familiar hum of laughter and clinking glasses filled Southern Roots, the local tavern where everyone came to unwind. At a corner table, Hannah and Tommy leaned in close, matching mischievous grins stretched across their faces.

"I can't believe it's happening," Hannah said, her voice hushed but eager. "Luke and Emma are back in the same town, working on the gazebo and Founder's Day prep together. It's like the universe is practically begging us to intervene."

Tommy nodded, setting his drink down with a smirk. "Yeah, they just need a little push. You should've seen the way Luke lit up when I mentioned Emma. The guy's got it bad, even if he doesn't realize it yet."

"And Emma's just as bad," Hannah added, rolling her eyes affectionately. "She tries to act all professional whenever she talks about him, but you can tell she's still got feelings. I mean, who wouldn't? Luke was her first love, after all, but I just think she's having trouble believing second chances do happen."

Just then, the door swung open, and in walked Luke, fresh from the day's work, looking surprised to see them but pleased. "Well, if it isn't my two favorite troublemakers," he said, pulling up a chair.

"Hey, look who decided to show up," Tommy said, exchanging a quick glance with Hannah. "We were just...talking about you."

Luke raised an eyebrow, but his grin was easy. "Is that so? And what have I done to deserve the honor of being the topic of conversation?"

"Oh, nothing," Hannah said, feigning innocence. "Just a little... observation. You know, about how nice it must be to be back in town, getting the old gazebo fixed up, reconnecting with some folks."

"Uh-huh." Luke leaned back, sensing the not-so-subtle undertones but playing along. "And who exactly am I reconnecting with?"

Tommy laughed. "Don't act clueless, Luke. We saw you walk Emma down the street earlier. Looked like a nice little stroll."

"Yeah," Hannah chimed in, "we're just saying, maybe fate has a hand in putting the two of you back together."

Luke gave a half-smile, shaking his head. "You two are relentless, you know that? We're just... old friends."

"Friends, huh?" Tommy nudged him. "Remember, we were both first hand witnesses to your love story in high school, so we know better. And, 'friends' don't explain the look on your face when I mentioned her name earlier?"

Luke hesitated, glancing between his friends. "Look, I'm here to do a job, nothing more. If Emma's around, well, that's just part of the deal."

Hannah leaned in, her grin widening. "You keep telling yourself that, Luke. Meanwhile, we'll be here, making sure you two get plenty of... opportunity."

Luke chuckled, a little wariness mixed with intrigue in his eyes. "Should I be worried about this?"

"Nah," Tommy said, patting his shoulder. "Just think of us as ... little helpers. You'll thank us one day."

As the night wore on, Luke couldn't shake the feeling that maybe, just maybe, his friends were onto something. And as he left Southern Roots, he realized he didn't mind the thought as much as he thought he would.

Chapter Three
Hidden Truths and New Deals

EMMA WIPED HER HANDS on a napkin, the smell of homemade casseroles and fresh bread wafting through the church hall. The annual church potluck was in full swing, and she was doing her best to stay focused on conversations about sweet potato pie and deviled eggs instead of the growing tensions in her life.

Luke had been avoiding her all afternoon, but she could feel his presence just across the room, where he was chatting with Tommy. Her heart tugged again, remembering their earlier conversation and the way his eyes had darkened when he'd hinted at things left unsaid.

Across the room, she spotted a familiar face—one she hadn't seen in years. Dressed in a tailored suit and sporting a Rolex, Kevin Pollard stood out among the crowd like a peacock in a barnyard. The nerd from high school who everyone used to ignore had transformed into a successful real estate developer. And judging by the confident look on his face, he wasn't just here for the potluck.

Kevin caught her eye and smiled, making his way toward her. Emma braced herself.

"Emma Thompson," he said smoothly, holding out his hand. "It's been a long time."

"Kevin," she replied, taking his hand. "It has been a while. You look... well."

He chuckled, glancing around the room. "I see Carter's Creek hasn't changed much. It's quaint. I always liked it here."

"Quaint." Emma resisted the urge to roll her eyes. That was one way to describe the place she'd worked so hard to preserve. "What brings you back?"

Kevin's smile widened. "I'm working on a new project, and I wanted to discuss it with you. Over dinner, perhaps? It's a business deal. I'm looking to purchase a large plot of land near the square, but I'll need the mayor and town council on board for the rezoning. I thought you might be interested in hearing my pitch."

Emma raised an eyebrow. This wasn't the first time a developer had come sniffing around town, but something about Kevin's offer felt unsettling. Still, she couldn't refuse outright. The town's future was in her hands, and she needed to at least hear him out.

"I suppose dinner could work," she replied cautiously. "I'd need to discuss the deal with the council, of course."

Kevin's grin widened, his eyes sweeping over her in a way that made her skin crawl. "Of course. But I think we can work out something mutually beneficial."

Emma forced a smile, though the moment left a sour taste in her mouth.

***

HIDDEN TRUTHS AND NEW DEALS

Across the room, Linda was busy stirring the pot, leaning over to Tommy with a sly grin. Her bleach-blonde hair teased into soft curls, Linda had always been the type to flaunt her assets, and she wasn't shy about it. Now in her early 40s, recently divorced, she'd set her sights on securing a new man—or a good time. And today, she had her eyes on Kevin Pollard.

"You know, Kevin's taking the mayor to dinner," she whispered loud enough for half the table to hear. "Bet they're not just talking business."

Tommy smirked. "You think? He was a geek back in the day. But I guess money changes things."

Linda leaned back, her lipstick-smudged grin widening. "Oh, I'm sure Emma's all business, but Kevin's got that look. And I've got my eye on him."

At that moment, Luke stepped over, catching the tail end of Linda's gossip. "What's that about Kevin and Emma?"

Linda's eyes gleamed as she spotted an opportunity. "Word is, he's taking her to dinner to talk about rezoning that land by the square. But between you and me, I think he's got more than business on his mind."

Luke's jaw tightened, and he shot a glance across the room where Emma was talking with Kevin. The sight of them together sent a jolt through him. Linda, noticing his reaction, took the opportunity to slide closer.

"You got your eye on Kevin too, Luke?" she teased, batting her eyelashes.

Luke's gaze shifted back to Linda, and an idea began to form. He wasn't the jealous type, but something about Kevin didn't sit right with him. If he couldn't stop Emma from having dinner with the guy, maybe he could keep an eye on him.

"What do you say we have dinner the same night Kevin's taking Emma out?" Luke suggested, his voice smooth. "That way you can keep your eye on him and make your move."

Linda's eyes lit up, clearly thrilled at the prospect of getting her chance with Kevin while having Luke on her arm. "A date with you and a chance to steal Kevin away? Count me in."

Luke gave her a half-hearted grin, knowing his motives were far from what Linda thought. This wasn't about romance—it was about making sure Kevin Pollard didn't pull anything shady with Emma.

***

The night of the dinner came quickly. Luke and Linda met at Southern Roots, where they sat at a small table near the bar, just close enough to see the back dining room where Kevin and Emma had been seated. Linda was practically glowing with excitement, her dress tight enough to turn heads, and her perfume strong enough to knock over anyone too close. She was playing the part, and Luke couldn't help but appreciate her confidence, even if his mind was elsewhere.

"So," Linda said, leaning closer, "you think Kevin's gonna make his move tonight?"

Luke's eyes flicked toward the back, watching Emma sit across from Kevin. "I don't trust him."

Linda smirked. "Don't worry. I'll make sure he knows he's not the only one in town with options."

As Linda reached for her wine glass, Luke's father, Tom Hunter, appeared from the back kitchen, wiping his hands on his apron. He ran the tavern with an iron fist, but tonight he looked more amused than anything as he approached the table.

"Well, well," Tom said, raising an eyebrow. "Didn't expect to see you here with Linda. Thought you were keeping to yourself these days."

Luke glanced at his father, forcing a grin. "Just keeping an eye on things."

Tom chuckled, but his eyes shifted toward Kevin and Emma in the back, clearly noticing where Luke's attention was focused. "Seems like you're more interested in what's happening back there."

Linda smiled sweetly, but her gaze was sharp as she cut in. "Luke's being a gentleman, Tom. Keeping me company while I keep my eye on that land-grabbing city boy back there."

Tom's face darkened slightly, his jaw tightening. "Pollard's been making noise about buying up land for years. If he gets his way, Carter's Creek will look more like one of those soulless developments than the place we've built. Better make sure he doesn't smooth-talk his way into anything."

Luke nodded. "I'm working on it."

As Tom walked away, Linda leaned in, lowering her voice. "You know, Kevin's got his eye on the town, but I think it's Emma he really wants. You'd better figure out what you want before she gets swept up in all this."

Luke's eyes darkened at the thought, but before he could respond, the door to the back dining room opened, and Emma and Kevin stepped out. Kevin had that same smug smile plastered on his face, while Emma's expression was unreadable.

Linda straightened, her lips curving into a seductive smile. "Show time."

As Kevin and Emma approached, Luke stood, his eyes locking onto Kevin's. "You guys done talking business?" he asked casually.

Kevin's smile didn't falter. "For now. But there's more to discuss." He glanced at Emma, who gave Luke a small, tight smile before turning toward the door.

"I'll catch up with you later," Emma said to Luke, her voice quiet but firm.

Luke watched them leave, his fists clenching at his sides. Linda leaned closer, whispering in his ear. "If you want her, you'd better make your move. Guys like Kevin don't wait around."

***

Later that night, Emma found herself walking back toward her loft. It was late, and the streets were quiet as she made her way across the square, past the broken gazebo, and toward the bakery where she lived in the loft above her best friend's shop. The air was cool, the kind of night that felt peaceful but heavy at the same time.

She heard footsteps behind her and turned to see Luke catching up. She hadn't expected to see him again tonight, but here he was, his face tense, eyes serious.

"Emma, wait."

She stopped, her heart pounding for reasons she didn't fully understand. "Luke, what are you doing?"

He stood a few feet away, hands shoved in his pockets, looking like he was struggling with what to say. "I needed to talk to you. After everything tonight... I couldn't let you walk away without saying this."

Emma crossed her arms, bracing herself. "Saying what?"

Luke hesitated, his gaze dropping for a moment before he looked back at her, his voice steady but softer than usual. "I didn't leave because I didn't care about you. I left because I didn't think I was enough. My dad, this town... I couldn't breathe here. I thought if I stayed, I'd drag you down with me. I thought I was doing the right thing by leaving."

Emma blinked, the weight of his words settling heavily. "So now what? You think we can just... be friends?"

Luke's expression tightened, as if the question itself hurt. "I don't know. But I don't want things to stay like this. I know we can't go back. I'm just hoping we can move forward. Maybe as friends, neighbors. Whatever it is, I need us to at least clear the air."

Emma hesitated, sensing there was more to the story, something Luke wasn't saying. She glanced back toward the church, feeling the weight of her father's expectations all those years ago. Maybe there was more to why Luke had left, but now wasn't the time to ask.

"We'll see," Emma said cautiously. "I'm not sure we can be friends, Luke. But we both have to live here, and we'll have to figure that out."

Luke nodded, a flash of hope in his eyes despite her hesitation. "That's all I'm asking. Let's just... take it one step at a time."

Emma sighed, turning toward her loft. "Good night, Luke."

As she walked away, Luke stood there, hands shoved back into his pockets, watching her disappear into the quiet night. He didn't know what would happen next, but for now, just being on speaking terms felt like a step in the right direction. But as he stood there, he couldn't shake the feeling that there was something more—something he hadn't told her yet. And maybe, when the time was right, he'd finally tell her the full truth.

Chapter Four
Lingering Questions

EMMA SAT AT THE corner table in the tavern, absentmindedly twirling her drink coaster between her fingers. Her mind was a whirlpool of confusion, pulling her deeper into thoughts about Luke, the late-night walk, and the way he looked at her like nothing had changed. But everything had changed, hadn't it?

Across the table, Hannah raised an eyebrow, watching Emma with an amused expression. "Okay, spill it. You've been a million miles away since I sat down."

Emma blinked, pulling herself back to the present. "Sorry, I'm just... thinking."

Hannah smirked. "About Luke, I'm guessing?"

Emma sighed, leaning back in her chair. "Yeah. We talked last night, after Kevin left. He walked me home."

Hannah leaned forward, intrigued. "And?"

"And... I don't know. He said things, things that made sense, but... I'm not sure I need those kinds of complications right now. My life is fine the way it is, right?!"

Hannah gave her a knowing look. "Fine? Sure. But is it really?"

Emma frowned, her fingers still twisting the coaster. "I've worked so hard to get to where I am. I don't need Luke coming back and throwing everything into chaos again. I don't even know if I can trust him. What if he leaves again?"

Hannah softened, her tone more serious now. "Look, I get it. But you've always been drawn to him. Maybe you just need to figure out what that means for you."

Emma bit her lip. There was no denying that something still pulled her toward Luke, but after all this time, she wasn't sure what she felt anymore. Part of her wanted to let the past stay in the past, but the other part... well, that part wasn't so easy to ignore.

Just as Emma was about to respond, the tavern door swung open, and the room seemed to shift. A tall, broad-shouldered man stepped inside, and Emma felt the air in the room change. His dark hair was a bit tousled, his square jaw covered in the slightest hint of stubble. He moved with a quiet confidence, like he was completely comfortable in his own skin. His green eyes swept over the room, taking everything in with an easy, assessing gaze.

Hannah nudged Emma, her eyes widening slightly. "Is that...?"

Emma nodded slowly. "Yeah. That's him. The new guy. Gabe. I met him briefly when he arrived in town a couple of days ago."

Hannah's lips parted in surprise. "I hear he's the new bartender, just moved to town. Well, now I understand why the gossips have been buzzing about him. He's... something."

Emma couldn't help but agree. Gabe was the kind of man who turned heads without trying. There was something rough around the edges about him, something that made it clear he wasn't from around here, and yet he carried himself with a calm, collected air. He wasn't loud or flashy, but his presence demanded attention.

"I've heard bits and pieces," Emma said, watching Gabe as he made his way to the bar. "Apparently, he came from the city, but no one knows why he ended up here. Mysterious, to say the least."

Hannah's gaze lingered on him, and Emma noticed the way her best friend sat up a little straighter, her eyes brightening with curiosity. "He doesn't look like the small-town type," Hannah said thoughtfully. "I wonder what brought him here."

Emma grinned, nudging her. "Maybe you should ask him yourself."

Hannah flushed slightly. "Yeah, right. I'm sure he's swamped with attention already."

Emma couldn't deny that. Ever since Gabe had arrived in town, the gossip mill had been working overtime. Ms. Beatrice and her crew had already speculated about his background—everything from an ex-cop on the run to a millionaire hiding out from the world. But Gabe wasn't offering any answers, keeping his past tightly wrapped in mystery.

"You know," Hannah said quietly, almost to herself, "it's nice to have a bit of mystery around here. Everyone else is so... predictable."

Emma followed Hannah's gaze, her curiosity growing. She didn't know much about Gabe beyond the rumors, but he certainly didn't blend into the background like most newcomers. There was a weight to him, something unspoken in the way he carried himself, like a man who had seen more than he let on.

Before Emma could say more, Gabe turned from the bar, his eyes scanning the room until they landed on Hannah. His green eyes held hers for a moment, a brief flicker of recognition passing between them. There was a warmth in his gaze, something subtle but undeniable.

Hannah quickly looked away, her cheeks flushing pink. "Oh God, he saw me staring."

Emma laughed softly. "I don't think he minded."

***

Luke worked quietly at the town square, sanding down a piece of wood on the gazebo. The rhythmic motion of the sandpaper against the wood should have been soothing, but his mind was anything but calm.

His thoughts kept drifting back to last night, to the way Emma had looked at him as they stood in the quiet night air, her eyes searching his for answers he wasn't sure he had.

He sighed, running a hand through his hair. What had he expected? That one conversation would undo years of hurt? That he could just walk back into her life and pick up where they'd left off?

"Crap," he muttered, tossing the sandpaper aside.

Part of him wanted to forget about the whole thing, to move on like he'd been trying to for years. But another part of him—the part that had always longed for Emma—couldn't let go. It was like she had a hold on him, even now.

As he worked, his father, Tom, strolled by, his hands in his pockets. "Still at it?" Tom said, nodding toward the half-finished gazebo panel. "Looks like it's coming together."

Luke shrugged, avoiding his father's gaze. "At least this is. "

Tom studied him for a moment, then leaned against the gazebo railing. "You've been different since you got back. More restless."

Luke frowned, not sure how to respond. "I've got a lot on my mind."

Tom chuckled, a dry, knowing sound. "Yeah, I bet you do. Saw you walking Emma home last night."

Luke's hands stilled on the wood, his chest tightening. "It wasn't anything. Just making sure she got home safe."

Tom raised an eyebrow. "You really expect me to believe that? I know what's between you two. It's always been there. Even when you were too young to understand it."

Luke exhaled, rubbing the back of his neck. "Doesn't matter now. Too much has happened. I messed things up."

Tom shook his head. "You didn't mess anything up. You left because you thought you had to. The question is, do you still believe that?"

Luke didn't answer, but his mind was racing. Did he still believe he had to stay away from Emma? Or was he just scared of what it would mean if he tried to stay?

***

Linda leaned against the polished bar, sipping her drink as she spotted a familiar face coming through the door. Her lips curved into a slow smile as she recognized him. "Well, as I live and breathe—Kevin Pollard, in the flesh. Are you meeting anyone here, honey?"

Kevin looked over, an eyebrow raised, clearly taken by surprise. "Nope. Just stopped in for a drink."

"Well then, come on over here and let's catch up for a few," she drawled, patting the seat next to her. "Buy me a drink, would you?"

They moved to a table near the front of the tavern, overlooking the town square. Through the large window, they could see Luke working on the gazebo, his shoulders tense as he sanded down the weathered wood. Linda noticed Kevin's gaze lingering on Luke, his expression unreadable.

She leaned back in her chair, adjusting her top just so as she crossed her legs, her lips curling into a smirk as she caught Kevin's lingering gaze on the scene outside. "You're keeping an eye on him, aren't you?"

Kevin didn't bother to deny it, his eyes fixed on Luke as he worked, his expression darkening ever so slightly. "I'm keeping an eye on everything. Always do."

Linda chuckled, her voice low and smooth. "Of course you do," she purred, tracing the rim of her glass with one manicured finger. "That's what I like about you, Kevin. You never miss a beat."

Kevin turned his attention back to her, his gaze calculating but with the faintest hint of a smile. "You know, Linda, you've been helpful in more ways than one."

Linda's smile widened, and she leaned in, her fingers lightly trailing along the edge of her glass, her eyes gleaming. "Well, I do enjoy being helpful. And if there's anything else I can... assist you with, don't hesitate to ask."

Kevin let out a low chuckle, shifting his attention back toward Luke outside, his eyes narrowing slightly. "Oh, I'm sure something will come up."

Linda's gaze followed his, her eyes flickering with a spark of mischief as she considered the scene outside. She leaned back, raising her glass in a mock toast. "I'm sure," she murmured, her voice layered with amusement.

For a moment, they sat in comfortable silence, both seemingly lost in their own thoughts, but the shared look between them spoke volumes. In a town as small as Carter's Creek, alliances were everything, and Linda knew exactly where she stood. She was in it for the fun—and maybe just a bit of trouble.

Chapter Five
A Walk Down Memory Lane

THE FOUNDER'S DAY COMMITTEE meeting buzzed with the energy of volunteers, their voices mixing with the occasional rustle of papers. Emma sat at the head of the table, her coffee warm in her hands, listening to the chatter as people settled into their seats. Across from her, Hannah and Tommy shared a look, one that immediately put Emma on alert.

"So," Hannah said, breaking into the discussion with a purposeful smile, "Emma and Luke, how about you two map out the parade route and take note of what needs fixing along the way?"

Emma raised an eyebrow, glancing between them suspiciously. "Us? Really?"

Tommy grinned, nudging Luke's shoulder with an easy-going laugh. "Who better, right? I mean, you're the mayor, and Luke's already got his hands on the gazebo. You two know this town better than anyone. And besides, it'll be a quick walk."

"Quick walk?" Emma repeated, crossing her arms. "This sounds like a setup."

"Oh, don't be so dramatic," Hannah replied, giving Emma an innocent look. "Think of it as... delegation. We're just making sure the parade route gets the best possible inspection."

Luke chuckled from his spot leaning against the back wall, clearly amused. "I'm game if you are," he said, casting Emma a lopsided smile that only deepened her suspicions.

She sighed, giving Hannah and Tommy a hard look. "You two aren't fooling anyone, you know."

Hannah blinked, feigning innocence. "Fooling? Us? Come on, Emma, this is purely professional. Besides, you'll want someone reliable checking out that route, right?"

Emma exhaled, glancing around at the rest of the committee, most of whom were looking away or fighting back grins. She knew she was backed into a corner. "Alright," she said, leveling her gaze at Luke. "We'll handle it. But only if Luke can actually stay focused on the task."

"Oh, I'll be focused," Luke replied smoothly, his eyes glinting with amusement. "Lead the way, boss."

Hannah suppressed a laugh, and Tommy saluted the two of them with his coffee cup. "There you go, problem solved. Just keep us posted if you two get lost along the way."

Emma rolled her eyes, shifting her focus back to the meeting agenda. "Fine, but just know I'll remember this. Now, if we're done assigning my workload..."

Tommy grinned, not the least bit apologetic. "Hey, we're just here to help."

As the meeting continued, Emma caught Luke smirking from across the table, and she knew without a doubt that Hannah and Tommy weren't done playing matchmaker. But she'd go along with it—just this once.

***

The sun was dipping lower, casting a warm, golden glow over Carter's Creek as Emma and Luke strolled side by side through the quiet streets, pointing out areas in need of repairs or decorations. Their footsteps echoed softly, blending with the sounds of distant birds and the occasional creak of an old sign swaying in the evening breeze. Each step seemed to stir up memories, filling the silence between them with unspoken thoughts.

As they neared the park, Luke slowed, a smile tugging at his lips. "Remember the summer fair they used to hold here?"

Emma grinned, unable to resist the flood of memories. "How could I forget? You spent all your tickets trying to win that giant teddy bear, then immediately dropped it in the mud."

Luke laughed, his eyes twinkling. "In my defense, that thing was bigger than both of us combined. And if I remember correctly, I offered to carry you home instead of the bear."

Emma shook her head, laughing. "Sure, and then you disappeared halfway home because you and Tommy decided to climb up on the water tower for a 'better view' of the town."

Luke rubbed the back of his neck, looking sheepish. "Okay, that was a bit reckless, I'll admit. But hey, Tommy and I had to uphold our reputation as local troublemakers."

They both laughed, the tension between them easing as memories wrapped around them like a comfortable old blanket. It felt like old times, like they'd slipped back to being carefree teenagers again.

As they continued walking, Emma's gaze drifted to the gazebo, its newly sanded wood gleaming in the fading light. She couldn't help but smile. "Do you remember the 4th of July when you tried to impress everyone by setting off your own fireworks?"

Luke groaned, shaking his head with a grin. "Oh, don't remind me. One of those rockets shot straight toward the mayor's car."

Emma burst out laughing. "And you tried to blame it on Tommy! Poor guy was grounded for two weeks."

Luke chuckled, shaking his head. "It worked, though! I got off with just a warning. Tommy was furious—he still brings it up every now and then, just to remind me."

Emma wiped a tear from her eye, still giggling. "You two were so ridiculous. It's a miracle you both survived your teenage years with the stunts you pulled."

Luke shrugged, his smile softening. "What can I say? Small towns bring out the troublemaker in you. But we did have fun, didn't we?"

They fell into a comfortable silence as they walked, the laughter lingering between them. As they reached the edge of the square, they stopped by the old oak tree, its sturdy trunk carved with countless initials. Luke's gaze softened as he traced a set of faded letters, a wistful look in his eyes.

"Our initials are still here," he murmured, brushing his fingers over the weathered carving. "Back then, I thought this would last forever—you, me, and our plans to take on the world."

Emma's smile faltered, her gaze fixed on the initials they'd carved so many years ago. "We were just kids, Luke. It was a long time ago."

He nodded, his tone quieter. "Yeah. But it was good while it lasted, wasn't it?"

Before Emma could reply, the sound of footsteps broke the stillness. She looked up to see Kevin and Linda strolling toward them, both wearing smug expressions that made Emma's stomach turn. Linda's smile widened as she took in the scene before her.

"Well, isn't this cozy?" Linda drawled, her gaze flicking between Emma and Luke with thinly veiled amusement.

Emma straightened, her tone steady. "Just doing what the committee asked—planning the parade route."

Kevin folded his arms, his gaze shifting from Emma to Luke with a knowing smile. "So that's what you're calling it?"

Luke crossed his arms, mirroring Kevin's stance, though his smile was anything but friendly. "Yeah, that's exactly what we're doing."

Linda leaned in toward Kevin, her eyes glinting with barely disguised mischief. "Sure looks like more than just planning to me."

Emma narrowed her eyes, refusing to let Linda's insinuations get under her skin. "If you have a problem with how we're handling things, feel free to bring it up with the committee."

Before Kevin could respond, more footsteps approached. Hannah and Tommy appeared around the corner, acting as though they'd just stumbled upon the group.

"There you are!" Hannah called, hurrying over, her voice laced with urgency. "We need you both—now."

Tommy clapped Luke on the shoulder with a grin. "C'mon, man. There's a... situation we need you both for."

Emma and Luke exchanged a quick look of relief before allowing their friends to steer them away, leaving Kevin and Linda behind. As they walked, Emma glanced back, catching the frustrated look on Linda's face and couldn't help but smile. For once, Hannah and Tommy's scheming had come in handy.

***

Inside Southern Roots, the tavern's warm lights and rustic décor wrapped around them like a familiar hug. Gabe stood behind the bar, polishing a glass and grinning as Emma, Luke, Hannah, and Tommy walked in.

"Afternoon," Gabe greeted them, his tone cheerful. "Looked like you all could use a break."

Emma shook her head, a smile tugging at her lips. "Alright, what's the emergency?"

Hannah exchanged a look with Tommy, grinning slyly. "No emergency—just figured you could use a rescue."

Tommy chuckled, nudging Luke. "Yeah, man, you owe us one."

Luke laughed softly. "Yeah, thanks for that. Perfect timing, as usual."

They settled into a booth near the window, the tension from the run-in with Kevin and Linda beginning to lift. As they relaxed, it felt like slipping into an old rhythm, like they were kids again, plotting adventures and mischief together.

"So," Hannah started, leaning forward with a mischievous grin, "remember that time we got stuck in the church basement during that storm? Luke thought it'd be a fantastic idea to climb up the old bell tower."

Tommy snorted, shaking his head. "Still have nightmares about that ladder breaking. Thought we'd all end up stranded in there forever."

Luke chuckled, taking a sip of his drink. "Hey, I was going to save us all with my rope-swinging skills. You just didn't believe in my plan."

Emma rolled her eyes, a playful smirk on her face. "And we all ended up soaked because your 'rope-swinging' landed you squarely in the baptismal pool. I'm still mad about how cold that water was."

The whole table erupted in laughter, their voices filling the room as they relived the old story. Gabe, leaning over the bar with a grin, chuckled along with them, nodding listening to their memories. For a few moments, the years seemed to melt away, the connection between them as effortless as ever, and Gabe could feel the depth of their friendships from their warm memories.

But as the laughter began to fade, Tommy leaned forward, his expression shifting to something more serious. "All jokes aside," he said, lowering his voice, "what do you think Kevin's really up to?"

Hannah frowned, looking over at Emma. "He's been spending a lot of time with Linda lately. I don't like it. Whatever it is, it can't be anything good."

Emma nodded thoughtfully, her fingers tracing patterns on the table as she thought. "I don't trust him either. He's been pushing those zoning changes harder than usual. It's like there's something he's not telling the council."

At that, Gabe, who had been listening nearby, cleared his throat. He put down the glass he was wiping and walked over, resting his hands on the back of a nearby chair. "You're not wrong about that," he said quietly, glancing around to make sure no one else could hear.

The group turned to look at him, their curiosity piqued.

Gabe leaned in, his voice just above a whisper. "I overheard Kevin talking to someone the other day. He mentioned something about a big development deal—something that's supposed to change the town. And from what I could gather, it sounds like he's trying to push some permits through without attracting attention."

Emma's eyes narrowed, a steely look of determination coming over her. "So he's trying to do this under the radar."

Luke crossed his arms, his face darkening as he processed Gabe's words. "He's planning more than just a couple of shops, isn't he?"

Gabe nodded, his expression grim. "Yeah. From what I heard, it's big. Think... hotel-sized. This isn't just a small expansion; it's a complete change to the town's feel."

Hannah exchanged a worried glance with Emma. "If he manages to pull this off, Carter's Creek won't be the same. We need to figure out exactly what he's up to before it's too late."

Emma straightened, her mind already racing through possibilities. "Agreed. We'll need to look over the council records, see if there's anything we're missing. And Gabe, keep your ears open. Anything you hear could help."

Gabe gave her a firm nod. "You got it. I'll keep you posted."

They sat in silence for a moment, the weight of the revelation settling in. What had started as a simple stroll down memory lane had turned into something much more complicated. And as they exchanged determined looks, one thing was clear: whatever Kevin was planning, they weren't going to let it happen without a fight.

Chapter Six
Secrets, Schemes and Spilled Tea

KEVIN STROLLED INTO THE town hall, catching Emma just as she wrapped up a meeting with the council. His eyes gleamed with that signature charm that always left Emma feeling uneasy.

"Mayor Thompson," Kevin said smoothly, "Got a moment?"

Emma glanced at him, already bracing herself for another sales pitch. "Sure, Kevin. How can I help you?"

Leaning against the doorframe, Kevin's smile never wavered. "Wanted to run a few ideas by you. Big plans for Carter's Creek, you know? I think you'll like what you hear."

Emma folded her arms, skeptical. "Big plans for Carter's Creek? I definitely need to review your plan."

Kevin waved a hand, brushing off her concerns. "Businesses, jobs—things that'll make this town thrive."

Emma's eyes narrowed, her tone firm. "I'd have to see the development details to know that, Kevin. Our town's process for approving deals like this involves thorough review—impacts on the environment, benefits to Carter's Creek, and much more. If you're serious, you need to submit your plan."

Kevin's smile faltered slightly but quickly recovered. "You'll get the details when the time's right. But I was hoping we could... discuss this on a more personal level, too. Maybe over dinner?"

Emma's stomach twisted with discomfort. "Let's keep things professional. If you want my support, the right place to handle this is in town hall, with a proper submission of your plans. No shortcuts, no favors. Otherwise, you're not winning me over."

Kevin's smile didn't quite reach his eyes as he backed away. "We'll see, Emma. You'll come around."

As Luke passed Kevin in the hallway, Emma sighed, crossing her arms. "More of his land deal garbage. He's still being vague and evasive, like always. He should know me better than to think he can pull the wool over my eyes."

Luke paused, stepping closer, his protective instinct kicking in. "Kevin's a snake. Always has been. If he's hiding something, we need to figure out what it is."

For a moment, their eyes met, a familiar sense of unity settling between them—just like when they were kids, working on projects together. But this time, the stakes were higher. The future of Carter's Creek was on the line—and maybe something more.

Luke broke the silence, his voice low but steady. "I can put my ear to the ground, see what the town's saying about Kevin and his deal."

Emma nodded, her resolve hardening. "Perfect. And I'll reach out to other town officials in the cities where he's worked. They'll tell me what they know. If you help me figure this out, I'll owe you one. I need to get ahead of this before he steamrolls me."

Luke's eyes sparked with determination. "Owe me, huh? Alright, consider it a deal. We'll uncover whatever he's hiding, together."

As they strolled out of town hall together, Emma felt a warmth spread through her. Their friendship felt like it was getting back on track, and maybe that was enough. They'd always been friends, and if that was all it could be, she could live with that.

As they reached the street and began to part ways, Luke leaned in, dropping a light kiss on her forehead. "We were always a good team."

Emma smiled softly, feeling a flicker of something deeper, but pushing it aside. "Yeah, we were."

***

Later that evening, Luke and Tommy sat at their usual table in the tavern, beers in hand. The noise of the bar provided a backdrop to their conversation, but Luke's mind was elsewhere, silently processing how to uncover Kevin's plot.

Tommy took a long drink, then leaned back in his chair. "So, what's Kevin up to now? He's always lurking."

Luke sighed, rubbing a hand over his face before taking a sip of his beer. "He's sniffing around Emma. Trying to pull her into his land deal, but it's obvious he wants more than just her support. There's something off about this whole thing."

Tommy raised an eyebrow, his expression turning serious. "Still protective, huh? Some things don't change."

Luke chuckled softly, but the weight behind his words was clear. "I can't help it. She's... Emma. And Kevin's not up to anything good for Carter's Creek."

Tommy gave a nod, his expression thoughtful. "Kevin's always had that slimy edge. Emma's strong, though, but even the strongest need people backing them up. She needs to protect Carter's Creek, but also find a way to move it forward."

Luke's gaze grew distant for a moment. "I've always admired her strength. It's what drew me to her, even as kids. She's been fighting for this town for years, and I won't let her face this alone. We need to help her cut the head off that snake."

Tommy grinned, sensing the deeper feelings behind Luke's words. "You know, back in the day, you were so obvious about your crush on her. It was painful to watch. You had no poker face at all."

Luke laughed, shaking his head. "Yeah, I was a mess. Thought she was perfect."

Tommy leaned forward, his eyes gleaming with curiosity. "Still think she is?"

The question hung in the air, making Luke pause. He hadn't fully faced what being back here meant—being around her again, working together. His chest tightened, and he wasn't sure if it was nostalgia or something more.

"I don't know," Luke said finally, his voice quieter. "Being back, seeing her again... It's making me rethink everything. The town, the past, her."

Tommy clinked his beer bottle against Luke's with a grin. "Well, you'd better figure it out soon. Kevin's circling around, and if you're going to make a move, you need to do it before he complicates everything."

Luke's jaw tightened at the thought of Kevin's schemes. His mind was already spinning with ways to get ahead of whatever Kevin was planning. He wasn't going to let Emma face it alone—not again.

"I'm on it," Luke said, his voice resolute. "Kevin's not winning this one."

SECRETS, SCHEMES AND SPILLED TEA 47

Tommy nodded approvingly. "Good. But just remember, it's not only about stopping Kevin. If you're serious about Emma, you need to decide what you really want."

Luke didn't respond, but his mind was already working through that as well. He had a feeling this was about more than just Kevin's land deal—and he wasn't sure if he was ready for everything it could mean.

***

The next afternoon, Emma found herself running into Linda outside the diner. It wasn't intentional, but given Linda's involvement with Kevin, Emma figured it was a good opportunity to dig a little deeper.

"Linda," Emma called, waving her over. "Got a second?"

Linda turned, her smirk ever-present. "Emma! Of course. What's up?"

Emma hesitated for a moment before speaking. "I was wondering if you knew anything more about Kevin's plans. He's been talking in circles, and I don't like being kept in the dark."

Linda's smile widened, and she crossed her arms with a confident air. "Oh, I know plenty. But, you know, Kevin trusts me with... certain details. I'm like a vault—nobody gets anything out of me."

Emma smiled politely, hiding her amusement. "Of course, but if there's anything you can share... the town deserves to know what's going on."

Before Linda could respond, the familiar voices of Ms. Beatrice and Mabel floated over from the sidewalk nearby.

"Look at that," Ms. Beatrice whispered, though loudly enough for Emma and Linda to hear. "The Mayor and Linda, having a little chat. I wonder what secrets are being spilled now."

Mabel added with a grin, "Maybe they're talking about Kevin. That boy's got his hands in everything lately."

Linda puffed up slightly, pride in her voice. "Nothing gets out of me, ladies."

Ms. Beatrice smiled, her eyes gleaming. "That's what they all say, Linda. But secrets have a way of getting out."

As the gossips walked away, Linda turned back to Emma with a wink. "Don't worry. I'm like a vault."

Emma raised an eyebrow. "Of course."

Linda leaned in conspiratorially. "But, you know, between us, Kevin's planning something much bigger than he's letting on. Resorts, hotels, the works. He's already lined up investors. He plans to turn this place into a major hotspot. And, what Kevin wants, Kevin gets."

Emma's eyes widened, but she kept her tone neutral. "And he hasn't mentioned any of this to the council? A lot of infrastructure is necessary for plans like that."

Linda shook her head. "Nope. It's all under wraps for now. But don't worry, I'm not supposed to say a word."

Emma forced a smile. "Thanks, Linda. You're... quite the vault."

Linda leaned back, pleased with herself, but Emma's mind was racing. If Kevin was quietly planning something as massive as resorts and hotels, there would be huge consequences for the town. This was bigger than she thought, and Kevin's secrecy only made it worse.

Before Linda could say more, Emma pressed lightly. "What about the environmental impact? Those plans would need to go through strict approval processes."

Linda waved a hand dismissively. "Oh, Kevin's got everything covered. He's already thinking ahead. You don't need to worry about all that."

Emma bit her tongue, unwilling to push too hard just yet. "Good to know. Well, thanks for the heads-up, Linda."

As Linda walked off, Emma's expression shifted, concern furrowing her brow. She had to get ahead of this—Kevin was playing a bigger game than she'd realized, and now more than ever, she needed Luke's help to uncover the truth.

***

Later that night, as the tavern began to quiet down, Kevin was the last person in the bar, leisurely sipping his drink. Gabe wiped down the counter, keeping an eye on the developer, whose demeanor was as smug as ever.

"You've been busy lately," Gabe said casually, his tone light as he cleared some glasses.

Kevin glanced at him, eyes narrowing slightly. "Always am."

Gabe nodded. "Heard you're making some big moves. People around town are starting to wonder what's going on."

Kevin smirked, the corner of his mouth lifting as if amused. "Well, people love to talk. Especially about exciting developments."

Gabe leaned in just slightly, his tone staying casual. "So, are we getting new shops, or are you planning something bigger?"

Kevin's gaze shifted, a flash of calculation behind his eyes. "You could say there's more in the works than I'm letting on. This town's about to see a lot of changes."

Gabe raised an eyebrow, still playing along. "Sounds like big stuff. I'm pretty new to town, don't know how all of this works yet, but I'm glad to hear things are moving forward. What kind of changes are we talking about?"

Kevin's smile widened, but there was something cold in it. "Let's just say Carter's Creek is a diamond in the rough. Someone like me can make it shine. We're talking major developments—resorts, hotels, real estate expansions."

Gabe felt his pulse quicken slightly. This was more than he'd expected to get. "That's huge," he replied, keeping his tone interested. "So, you've got investors lined up?"

Kevin leaned back in his chair, his confidence growing. "Already got the backers I need. The real trick is pushing it all through without too much interference."

Gabe's mind raced. He had to tread carefully but push just enough. "Interference? You mean the town council?"

Kevin gave a short laugh. "Them? They're nothing. The real issue is keeping people like Emma on my side. The locals get attached to their little town traditions. But once they see the money rolling in, they'll change their tune."

Gabe nodded slowly, filing the information away. "Yeah, I guess money talks."

Kevin's smirk returned, his eyes glinting with arrogance. "Exactly. And I've got the kind of money this town's never seen. This place is going to be a hotspot, and no one's going to stop it."

Gabe kept his expression neutral, but inside he knew he had just heard something critical. "Sounds like you've got everything figured out."

Kevin shrugged, his smugness palpable. "I always do."

Gabe paused, weighing his next words carefully. "Must be risky, though. Big plans like that, you've got a lot riding on it."

Kevin's gaze hardened. "Curiosity can be dangerous, Gabe. Stick to pouring drinks."

With that, Kevin downed the rest of his drink and tossed some cash on the bar before heading for the door. Gabe watched him leave, the air in the tavern suddenly feeling heavy with the weight of what he'd just learned.

Gabe wiped the bar down one last time, his mind buzzing. Kevin's plans were bigger—and more dangerous—than anyone realized. And now he had something solid to take back to Emma and Luke. The town was in for a fight, and Gabe had just taken his first step toward figuring out how to stop Kevin from turning Carter's Creek into his personal playground.

Chapter Seven
Digging for the Truth

EMMA SAT AT THE large wooden desk in her office, the dim light from her desk lamp casting a soft glow over piles of paperwork. Luke sat across from her, flipping through town records, his brow furrowed in concentration. The silence between them was comfortable, but charged with something unspoken.

"This doesn't make sense," Emma muttered, tossing aside yet another document. "Kevin's been dancing around this development for months, and there's nothing here. No official requests, no paperwork, just... whispers."

Luke leaned back in his chair, his gaze softening as he watched her frustration build. "He's careful. Too careful. We both know he's hiding something."

Emma sighed, leaning her elbows on the desk, rubbing her temples. "But what? And why is he still trying to pull me into this? He knows I won't back something that isn't transparent."

Luke hesitated, then leaned forward, his voice low but firm. "What if we're looking in the wrong place?"

Emma frowned, sitting up straighter. "What do you mean?"

Luke flipped a page in the file he was holding, scanning it with sharp eyes. "Kevin's too smart to leave a direct trail. But what if the paper trail we need isn't in these proposals or development permits?"

Emma's brow furrowed, curiosity piqued. "Where, then?"

Luke paused, his eyes meeting hers with a spark of realization. "Property sales and transfers. If Kevin's been buying up land, he's doing it quietly—probably through shell corporations."

Emma's eyes widened, and she sat forward in her chair. "You think he's been using fake companies to cover his tracks?"

Luke nodded. "It's what I'd do if I wanted to hide what I was up to."

A slow smile spread across Emma's face, a glimmer of hope igniting in her chest. "Of course! We've been chasing his public moves, but the real action is probably happening behind the scenes. Property transfers—land deals done under the radar."

She reached for her computer, fingers flying across the keyboard as she accessed the town's property database. "We need to go back at least five years. Look for any land purchases or transfers around the areas Kevin's been eyeing for development."

Luke leaned over the desk, watching as Emma pulled up the records. "And we need to figure out what kind of names Kevin would use for these shell corporations."

Emma tapped her fingers against her chin, deep in thought. "Something generic but polished. He'd want it to sound legitimate. Maybe... Creekside Holdings? Riverfront Enterprises?"

Luke grinned. "Classic Kevin. Or maybe something with 'Global' in the name. You know, to make it sound bigger than it is."

Emma typed in a few keywords, cross-referencing property transfers with any corporations bearing those types of names. Her screen filled with results.

"There," she said, pointing at the screen. "Look at that—Creekside Ventures, a corporation that's bought up several small parcels around the town square. All purchased within the last few years."

Luke's eyes narrowed. "And I bet if we dig deeper, we'll find Kevin's fingerprints all over those deals."

Emma's pulse quickened, a rush of excitement cutting through her earlier frustration. "We've got him," she whispered, her eyes meeting Luke's. "We're finally on the right track."

A shared sense of victory surged between them. Without thinking, Emma jumped from her chair and flung her arms around Luke in a sudden, exuberant hug.

Luke blinked, caught off guard by the warmth of her body pressed against his, but his arms instinctively wrapped around her, pulling her closer for just a second. "We did it," he murmured, the closeness making his voice soft, almost intimate.

Realizing what she'd done, Emma quickly stepped back, her face flushed. She cleared her throat awkwardly, smoothing her hands over her blouse. "I—uh, sorry. I got a little... carried away."

Luke chuckled, stepping back too, though there was a faint smile tugging at the corner of his lips. "No problem. I get it. This is a big win."

They stood there for a beat, both a little more flustered than they'd like to admit. But the smiles that lingered on their faces weren't just about the investigation. There was something else—something unsaid but understood.

Emma was the first to break the silence. "We should... uh, plan our next move."

Luke nodded, trying to shake off the electric undercurrent. "Right. We need to see how far this Creekside Ventures reaches. Check if there are any other properties in or around town."

"And maybe I can reach out to some contacts in neighboring towns," Emma added, her voice regaining its steadiness. "See if Kevin's been pulling the same stunt elsewhere."

"Sounds good," Luke agreed, leaning against the desk, though his eyes still held a trace of that shared excitement. "We'll work together on this—partnership, right?"

"Right," Emma echoed, her heart still beating a little too fast. "Partnership."

But as they returned to their task, the smiles stayed. They knew they were on the verge of something—both in the investigation and perhaps with each other. But for now, they'd focus on helping the town... even if their hearts were already starting to race toward something else.

***

Luke pushed open the creaky door to Walker's Hardware & Supply store, the familiar smell of lumber, metal, and old paint welcoming him in. Tommy was behind the counter, scribbling down notes on an order form. He glanced up as the door chimed.

"Well, well, if it isn't the man of the hour," Tommy greeted with a grin, setting his pen down. "What brings you in? Need more nails, or is this a social visit?"

Luke walked up to the counter, leaning on it with a slight smirk. "Social visit. I need your eyes on something."

Tommy raised an eyebrow, intrigued. "Eyes, huh? What kind of trouble are we stirring up this time?"

Luke chuckled, shaking his head. "Nothing illegal, I promise. Just digging into Kevin's latest scam."

That piqued Tommy's interest. He crossed his arms and leaned back, nodding for Luke to continue.

"We've been going through property sales for the last few years. Emma and I found a couple of shell corporations—Creekside Ventures and some similar names—buying up land around town." Luke tapped his fingers on the counter, his expression serious. "The pieces are starting to fall into place, but we need more. Something concrete to tie Kevin to this mess."

Tommy nodded slowly, his brows knitting together. "Funny you mention that. I've had some weird shipments come through here lately. Supposedly for 'future development,' but it didn't make sense at the time. Big orders—construction materials—but no one's started a project that needs them. I figured it was Kevin."

Luke's interest sharpened. "What company name is on those orders?"

Tommy flipped open a folder on the counter, sifting through papers until he found the one he was looking for. He handed it over to Luke. "It's listed as 'Clearwater Holdings,' but that name didn't come up in your search, did it?"

Luke shook his head, his eyes scanning the details. "No, but it fits Kevin's pattern. Generic enough to fly under the radar but polished enough to sound legit."

Tommy leaned forward, glancing at the paper. "They've been making big orders—cement, steel beams, timber. This one's for a delivery, but check this out—there's no specific delivery address. Just says 'Future pickup.'"

Luke frowned, flipping the paper over. "Future pickup? So, they're stockpiling materials, waiting for the right time to strike."

Tommy nodded, but his expression turned serious. "The thing is, Luke, they've been ramping up these orders fast. If they've already ordered this much material, they're not planning on waiting long."

Luke's eyes narrowed as he stared down at the paperwork. "So they're moving faster than we thought."

"Looks that way," Tommy agreed. "If Kevin's ready to start building soon, we're running out of time to stop him."

Luke's mind raced. If Kevin was preparing to break ground on his project, it would be much harder to stop him once construction was underway. They needed to act now, before the town got swept into a deal they couldn't get out of.

"Emma needs to see this," Luke muttered, folding the papers and tucking them into his jacket. "This changes everything. We're going to have to move fast."

Tommy leaned forward, resting his elbows on the counter. "Emma's been a strong advocate for our town, but we've never had a threat at this level. I know this brings up a lot from the past, a lot of unresolved feelings..."

Luke stiffened slightly, caught off guard by the shift in tone. "What do you mean?"

Tommy gave him a steady look. "You left before a lot of things were settled between you two. You care about her, and this whole thing with Kevin is forcing you to face it. You can't separate the two. You've got to think about what happens after all this blows over."

Luke's jaw tightened, and he looked down at the papers in his hand. "I don't want to make things harder for her. She's already got enough to deal with."

Tommy nodded, his voice softening. "Agreed, we need to help Emma stop Kevin sooner rather than later. This can wait, it's waited this long."

Luke didn't respond, but his expression tightened as he took in Tommy's words. His mind, however, was clearly set—Kevin needed to be stopped.

***

Emma was back at her desk, staring at the property records she and Luke had been poring over earlier. Her mind raced, but her frustration only grew with every dead end. Kevin was always one step ahead—too slippery to catch. She let out a sigh and rubbed her temples, trying to shake off the tension.

The sound of the door opening made her look up. Luke walked in, balancing a brown paper bag in one hand and papers in the other. His expression was serious, but there was a warmth in his eyes that hadn't been there earlier.

"Brought something for you," he said, setting the bag on her desk. "Figured you might not have eaten."

Emma raised an eyebrow, curious. "What is it?"

Luke gave her a small smile. "Remember those chicken wraps from Lila's Deli? You used to get them when you were stressed out in high school. Especially during finals week, cramming for those AP college prep classes."

Emma blinked, momentarily caught off guard by the gesture. She had completely forgotten about those late nights when her mind was fried from studying for exams and finishing final projects. The fact that Luke remembered made her smile.

"You didn't have to do that," she said softly, her eyes softening.

Luke shrugged. "Figured we could both use a break. Plus, I've got more details we can discuss while we eat."

He unpacked the wraps, and for a moment, the tension between them eased. They ate quietly, letting the meal provide a brief respite from the weight of everything hanging over them.

After a few bites, Luke couldn't wait any longer. He set his food down and pulled out the papers he'd brought with him.

"Stopped by Walker's Hardware & Supply store," he said, pushing the papers toward her. "Turns out Tommy's had some unusual shipments come through lately. Big construction materials—cement, steel beams, timber—but no project in town that needs them."

Emma frowned, taking the papers. "No project?"

Luke shook his head. "Nope. And the orders were made by Clearwater Holdings and a few other names. We're not sure yet, but it looks like these could be Kevin's shell corporations."

Emma's eyes narrowed as she studied the documents. "So, if he's stockpiling materials, he's planning to break ground soon. He's moving faster than we thought."

"Exactly," Luke said, his tone grave. "We need to find out what Kevin's up to that makes him think he can start building so soon, before he's even filed the development paperwork."

Emma exhaled sharply, her frustration turning into a renewed sense of urgency. "He must be dealing under the table, since he definitely hasn't been aboveboard with his plans. Time to dig into the projects that have created Kevin's success. You know how he loves to brag—let's ask Gabe to see what he can get Kevin to spill over a drink at the tavern. Once I have towns and projects, it'll be easy to find out from other town leaders how those projects developed."

Luke nodded. "That's a good plan. Let's get Gabe on the phone."

Emma pulled out her phone, scrolling through her contacts before tapping Gabe's number. She set the phone on her desk, putting it on speaker.

The phone rang twice before Gabe's voice came through, sounding upbeat as usual. "Hey, Mayor! What's up?"

"Hey, Gabe," Emma said, glancing at Luke before continuing. "Are you somewhere private? We don't want the whole tavern hearing this."

There was a pause before Gabe's voice returned, quieter this time. "Yeah, I'm in the back office. No one can hear. What's going on?"

Luke jumped in. "Can you get him talking about his past projects? We think he'll love telling you about the projects that created his wealth."

Gabe's tone shifted slightly, more serious now. "You want me to get Kevin talking? No problem. I see him in the tavern pretty often. I can strike up a conversation the next time he's in."

Emma smiled, grateful for Gabe's willingness to help. "That'd be great. I know you're new to our town, but you're already becoming a part of the core. We've got to get Kevin's deal with our town figured out sooner rather than later. Anything you can find out about the past or now may help."

"Got it," Gabe said. "I'll keep it casual, but I'll see what I can get him to spill. I'll report back as soon as I know anything."

"Thanks, Gabe," Luke said. "We owe you one."

"Hey, anytime," Gabe replied, his tone light again. "I'll do my part to help the town. Talk soon."

Emma hung up, exchanging a look with Luke. "That's one piece of the puzzle in motion."

Luke nodded, feeling a renewed sense of determination. "Now we just need to put the rest together."

Emma leaned back in her chair, her mind already working on the next step. "I'll meet up with some Realtors who were involved in the land deals. They might have some clues we can use."

For a moment, their eyes locked, the tension between them palpable. While they both felt something stirring inside, that had to be put aside for now. The town's needs had to come first.

***

After his call with Emma and Luke, Gabe headed back to the bar. The late evening crowd had thinned out, leaving only a few regulars clustered together at a table near the back. The bar itself was mostly empty, except for Linda, sitting alone, nursing her drink. Her usual confidence seemed absent as she stared down at her glass, lost in thought.

Gabe approached, wiping his hands on a towel as he came around the bar. "Linda," he greeted her, leaning against the counter. "You okay? You don't look like yourself tonight."

Linda glanced up, her smile flickering but never fully forming. "Gabe, always the concerned bartender," she teased softly, though the usual spark in her voice was missing. "I guess I'm just thinking too much."

Gabe studied her for a moment. "That's not like you. Want to talk about it?"

She sighed, swirling her drink as her gaze shifted back to the ice in her glass. "Maybe. You're a bartender, right? If I can't trust you, who can I trust?"

Gabe chuckled. "That's what they say. I'm all ears."

Linda hesitated, her finger tracing the rim of her glass as she glanced around the room to make sure no one was within earshot. The regulars were too busy in their own conversation to pay attention. She leaned in slightly, lowering her voice.

"Kevin's been... different lately," she said, her voice barely above a whisper. "Something's off. He's keeping things from me, and it's making me nervous. I don't know what he's planning, but... it's not good."

Gabe leaned closer, keeping his tone casual. "What's he nervous about?"

Linda took a sip of her drink, debating how much to reveal. "The investors. He's been complaining that they're getting restless because the project hasn't started yet. He's under pressure, but he's not telling me everything. And when Kevin starts hiding things, it's usually bad news."

She paused, her eyes flicking up to meet Gabe's. "I thought I could snag him, you know? He's got money, ambition. But now..." She trailed off, biting her lip. "I don't know if I made the right choice. I've lived in Carter's Creek all my life. My family still has land here, a business. And Kevin... he's scaring me a little. I don't know what he might do if he decides I'm a problem."

Gabe's brow furrowed. "You think he'd turn on you?"

Linda let out a shaky breath, her hand trembling slightly as she set her glass down. "I don't know. But I've seen him desperate before, and it's not pretty. He's cut people out when they've crossed him. I'm starting to wonder if I've crossed him by asking too many questions."

Gabe leaned in slightly, his voice low but reassuring. "Listen, Linda. You've got a lot of friends in this town. Luke, Emma, Tommy—they'd all gladly help you if you're in over your head. You're not alone in this."

Linda glanced at him, her expression softening slightly. "You think so?"

"I know so," Gabe said firmly. "And we need all the information we can get to protect the town. If you've got something that can help, now's the time to share it. We're all in this together."

Linda gave him a half-hearted smile, though the fear in her eyes lingered. "I don't know, Gabe. I just wanted... security. But this? It feels like it's going to blow up in all our faces."

For a moment, the bar was quiet except for the low murmur of voices from the regulars in the back. Gabe could see that Linda was genuinely rattled, something he hadn't seen from her before.

"Well," Gabe said gently, "if you ever need to talk again, you know where to find me. And if you figure out what's really going on, let me know. Maybe we can keep you—and the rest of the town—out of whatever mess Kevin's stirring up."

Linda nodded, her smile weak but grateful. "Thanks, Gabe. I appreciate it."

As she finished her drink and stood to leave, Gabe's mind was already turning over how he'd share this new information with Emma and Luke. Whatever Kevin was up to, it was bigger—and more dangerous—than they'd thought. And now, even Linda was starting to realize the cost.

Chapter Eight
A Little Help From My Friends

GABE WIPED DOWN THE bar counter, keeping a casual eye on Kevin, who sat at the far end nursing a whiskey. Kevin had been coming by more frequently lately, and Gabe had a feeling it was time to dig a little deeper. Just as he was considering how to get Kevin talking, the tavern door swung open, and in walked Sadie, a tray of freshly made desserts in her hands.

"Hey there, Sadie!" Gabe greeted with a grin, nodding her way. "Right on time, as usual."

Sadie smiled back, setting the tray down on the bar and dusting off her hands. "Thought I'd drop off tonight's treats and see how things are going here. Can't have Southern Roots without a little sweetness, right?"

Gabe chuckled, glancing at the tray piled with her famous pastries "You know these are half the reason folks come back," he said, giving her an appreciative wink. "I'm not just sayin' that. People are starting to request your cinnamon rolls specifically."

Sadie laughed, a light blush coloring her cheeks. "Well, we aim to please." She glanced over at Kevin, noticing his rather focused expression as he eyed his drink, and gave Gabe a quick look that said, *What's his story?*

Kevin lifted his glass and acknowledged Sadie with a slight nod. "Sadie, right? Owner of the bakery across town?" His tone was polite but guarded.

"That's right," Sadie replied smoothly, her eyes bright with a friendly curiosity. "And you're Kevin Pollard. I've seen you around town a bit more often lately."

Kevin smirked, looking pleased with the attention. "Business brings me here. Got some big projects on the horizon."

"Good for you," she replied, a touch of curiosity in her tone as she leaned an elbow on the bar. "It's nice to see folks investing in the town's future."

Gabe saw his opportunity and slid a fresh drink over to Kevin, flashing a friendly smile. "So, sounds like things are going well for you, Kevin. Seems like you've been busy working on some big projects?"

Kevin's expression brightened, and he seemed to relax as he sipped his drink. "You could say that. It's all about knowing how to get things moving. People like to talk, but talk doesn't build anything—connections do."

"Must be quite the network you've got," Gabe replied with feigned admiration. "What kind of deals are we talking here?"

Kevin leaned back, a smug look crossing his face. "Big land deals. Profitable ones. You ever hear of Riverside Heights? Took that town from being a nobody's pit stop to a thriving upscale community. Real estate values tripled in less than five years. Sometimes you have to push people out of their comfort zones—used eminent domain on a few family farms there. Got them fair compensation, but now the town's got new life."

As Kevin continued, Sadie picked up her phone, pretending to scroll, but her gaze shifted to Gabe, catching his eye and signaling her quiet support. She was catching every word and sensed they were onto something.

Gabe nodded, keeping his tone casual. "Must take some serious know-how to pull off a transformation like that."

Kevin's chest puffed out slightly with pride. "It's not just know-how; it's about who you know. When you've got the right people in the right places, pesky regulations move a lot faster. Did something similar in Briarwood Estates. People were dragging their heels on historic district protections. I got those outdated buildings into the modern age, and the profits were rolling in in no time."

Sadie chose that moment to chime in, her tone light but curious. "Sounds like you've got a way of making those hoops disappear. How do you get around all that red tape?"

Kevin glanced her way, visibly enjoying the interest. "Well, when you've got experience and connections, there's always a way. Sometimes it just takes a little... persistence."

Gabe shot Sadie a subtle glance of encouragement. Kevin, feeling at ease, continued, his voice dripping with self-satisfaction.

"Then there was Silver Creek Development—one of my biggest successes. Took an old industrial park and turned it into luxury condos and retail. Got the permits cleared in record time. City officials? They love to say yes when the dollars start flowing into their coffers."

"Bet the investors are thrilled with returns like that," Gabe added casually.

Kevin's eyes glinted as he finished off his drink. "Oh, they're all in. They know how I operate and know I get results. It's just a matter of time before Carter's Creek gets the same treatment."

Sadie, glancing over at Gabe, caught the steely look in his eyes and realized how serious this was. It wasn't just small-town gossip; Kevin had big plans, and they were about to shake up Carter's Creek.

Gabe leaned back, his gaze steady on Kevin. "Well, Kevin, here's to big dreams. Can't wait to see how things turn out."

As Kevin ordered another drink, Sadie and Gabe exchanged a silent look—one that promised this wasn't the end of their discussion.

***

As Kevin made his way to the tavern door, he met Linda coming in, his eyes narrowing with a dangerous gleam. Sadie, who had been standing by a nearby table, noticed the shift in his posture and turned her attention subtly, catching the tense exchange between them.

"Linda," Kevin said, his voice low and edged with a hint of menace, "you'd better mind your own business if you know what's good for you."

Linda froze, her confident demeanor fading as her face paled. "I... I wasn't trying to—"

"Good." Kevin interrupted, leaning in just enough to make his point clear. "Keep it that way."

Without waiting for a response, he turned and strode out, leaving the tavern in silence. Linda stood motionless by the entrance, visibly shaken, and Sadie's concern grew as she watched Linda take a deep breath before walking slowly toward the bar. Her shoulders were slumped, and the usual sparkle in her eyes had dulled to a shadow of worry.

Sadie slipped over to the bar and took a seat beside her as Gabe, noticing Linda's shaken state, slid over a fresh drink. "Here, this one's on me," he said, his tone gentle as he offered her a reassuring smile.

Linda's hand trembled as she reached for the glass, managing a grateful nod. "Thanks, Gabe," she murmured, blinking quickly to hold back tears. "I thought... I thought I could handle it, but Kevin—he's something else. I need to be smart about this before I'm in too deep."

Sadie placed a comforting hand on Linda's arm, her voice soft and steady. "You don't have to go through this on your own, Linda. We're here to help."

Linda stared into her drink, her voice barely above a whisper. "I thought I could work out this deal without getting too close. But now... now I'm realizing Kevin isn't the kind of guy you just say no to." She swallowed, looking from Sadie to Gabe with a flicker of fear in her eyes.

Gabe leaned forward, meeting her gaze with quiet assurance. "You've got friends here, Linda. People who have your back. Sometimes you just need to remember who's really looking out for you."

Linda managed a faint smile, the gratitude in her eyes tempered by lingering fear. "Thanks, Gabe. I really appreciate it. And you too, Sadie," she added, giving Sadie's hand a quick squeeze before glancing down at her unfinished drink. "But I think I need to head home and clear my head."

Pushing the glass away, she stood, her movements still a little shaky. "I appreciate you both. More than you know," she said softly, before heading to the door.

Sadie watched Linda leave, her face etched with worry. As the door swung shut behind Linda, she turned to Gabe, her voice low and serious. "We need to talk."

Gabe nodded, his expression matching her concern. "Absolutely. Let's wait until the place clears out. We need a plan."

***

As the last of the regulars make their way out, and Linda already on her way home, Gabe finished wiping down the counter and made his way over to Sadie, who was still seated at the bar.

Gabe leaned in, keeping his voice low. "I've got to level with you, Sadie. Emma and Luke asked me to get more details out of Kevin. That's why I've been digging."

Sadie raised an eyebrow, a smirk tugging at her lips. "So that's why you were asking him so many questions!"

Gabe chuckled softly, nodding. "Yeah, and thanks for helping me get him talking. He's been spilling more than I expected, but I'm afraid he's in deeper than we thought."

Sadie's expression grew serious. "I overheard him threatening Linda. He told her to stay out of his business, and she looked really shaken. She's in over her head, isn't she?"

Gabe's face darkened. "She is. Linda told me earlier that Kevin's got investors breathing down his neck, and she thought she could ride the wave and gain something, but she's realizing now that she's in too deep. He's moving fast, and if she knows too much, she's a liability."

Sadie frowned, nodding. "That explains why she was so scared tonight. We've got to get ahead of this."

Gabe reached for his phone. "We need to let Emma and Luke know everything. We can't wait."

He dialed Emma's number and waited as it rang. After a few moments, Emma picked up.

"Hey, Gabe. What's up?" Emma's voice came through the phone.

"We need to talk," Gabe said, glancing at Sadie. "Now if you can. I've got more on Kevin, and it's urgent."

"Perfect timing," Emma replied. "Luke, Tommy, Hannah, and I are working on the gazebo right now, but we can wrap up."

"Can you guys come over to the bar? It's closing time, so we'll lock it down and have the place to ourselves. We need to have a serious conversation."

Emma hesitated, then answered, "We'll be there in ten."

Gabe hung up, turning back to Sadie. "They're coming. We'll lay it all out tonight."

Sadie nodded, standing up and grabbing her jacket. "Good. Let's make sure we get everything out in the open, and unite the troops for Carter's Creek."

***

Gabe unlocked the door and quickly ushered Emma, Luke, Tommy, and Hannah inside, relocking it behind them. The dim lights and quiet of the empty tavern gave the room an unusual seriousness. Sadie, who'd been waiting by the bar, turned toward them, her face lighting up as she spotted her friend.

"Hannah!" Sadie greeted her with a smile, giving her a quick hug. "Didn't expect to see you this late—figured you'd be resting up for the bakery's early morning start."

Hannah grinned, returning the hug. "Trust me, I didn't expect to see you out so late either. You're usually the first one at the bakery, so what's keeping you out past closing time?"

Sadie laughed softly, a glint of worry in her eyes. "It's a long story. Let's just say I've been hearing things I couldn't ignore."

They broke apart, joining the rest of the group around a table, and Sadie took a breath, nodding to Emma and Gabe. Emma's brow furrowed, her voice low and serious as she glanced between Gabe and Sadie. "Alright, what's going on? You sounded pretty serious on the phone, Gabe."

Gabe leaned against the bar, his expression somber. "It's Kevin. He's a lot more dangerous than we thought. Sadie and I have been digging into his past, and turns out he's already made a name for himself. He's handled some big land deals where he used every trick in the book—some of them not exactly legal."

Sadie nodded, crossing her arms. "We're talking eminent domain abuse, forcing out families, and bulldozing historical districts. He's got a trail of projects where he's plowed through towns, leaving them unrecognizable."

Luke's jaw tightened as he crossed his arms. "And now he's here, planning the same thing for Carter's Creek."

Tommy leaned in, his voice low. "So what do we do? We can't just let him walk in and wreck the place."

Emma took a deep breath, steadying herself as she thought. "He's got to have someone on the council or in permits who's pushing this through. There's no way he'd get permits approved this fast without some help."

With a nod, Gabe reached into his pocket and pulled out a folded piece of paper, handing it to Emma. "Here's a list of the projects Kevin mentioned. Riverside Heights, Briarwood Estates, Silver Creek

Development—all places he's transformed. If we look into what happened in these towns, maybe we can find a pattern we can use against him."

Emma unfolded the paper, scanning the list before looking back at the group. "If we can connect what he did there to what he's planning here, we'll have the leverage we need."

Gabe's expression grew darker. "There's more. Linda's in trouble. She's involved, but Kevin's starting to see her as a liability. He threatened her tonight—told her to stay out of his business, and she's rattled."

Hannah's eyes widened as she turned to Sadie. "Linda? She always seems so put together."

Sadie shook her head. "Not this time. I overheard the whole exchange. Kevin's putting real pressure on her, and she admitted she's in over her head. She's terrified."

Luke clenched his jaw, his face hardening. "We can't wait any longer. We need to put a stop to this now."

Emma placed a calming hand on his arm, her tone measured. "We will, but we have to be smart about it. If we move too fast without proof, Kevin will spin it to his advantage. We need something concrete if we're going to stop him legally and protect Linda."

Tommy nodded. "Emma's right. We can't just charge in. But we need to act before he fast-tracks anything else through the council."

Gabe leaned back, crossing his arms thoughtfully. "Kevin's been bragging about how he's got everything lined up, like the permits are a done deal. He's got investors pressuring him to get this going ASAP. We've got to find out who on the council is in his corner."

Sadie leaned in, her gaze steady. "We already have a few leads on his past projects. If we can track down people from those towns and expose what he did, we can use that to stop him here."

Luke looked at Emma, his tone softer but determined. "You know people in neighboring towns. Do you think they'd talk if you asked?"

Emma nodded. "I'll reach out first thing tomorrow. We need all the information we can get."

Tommy turned to Luke, a knowing look in his eyes. "And we should dig into the council members, see if anyone's been pushing Kevin's agenda behind the scenes. There's got to be someone backing him."

Gabe gave a grim smile. "Sounds like we've all got work cut out for us."

Emma looked around the table, a feeling of gratitude swelling within her as she met each friend's determined gaze. "We're in this together. Kevin's not taking over this town."

Luke squeezed her shoulder gently, his voice soft but filled with resolve. "We've always been a good team."

The group sat in silence for a moment, letting the weight of their plan settle. Luke glanced down at the list of project names, then looked up at Emma and the group.

"I think I need to talk to my dad. He's seen enough to know who on the council might be involved, and he might have some insight on how Kevin's gotten this far already."

Emma nodded, her eyes determined. "Good idea. The more we know, the stronger we'll be."

And as they each turned their thoughts to the steps ahead, a shared sense of resolve filled the room. Whatever Kevin Pollard had in store, Carter's Creek wasn't going down without a fight.

Chapter Nine
Family Ties and Seeking Truth

LUKE SAT ON THE porch of his dad's house, the warm evening breeze carrying the sounds of crickets and distant voices from the heart of town. His dad leaned back in his chair, sipping coffee as he gazed out at the fading light. There was a comfortable silence between them, the kind that only years of shared history could build.

"I can't believe how much things are changing around here," Luke started, his voice low but steady. "It feels like the town's on the edge of something big—Kevin's pushing hard, and if we don't stop him... Carter's Creek might never be the same."

His dad nodded, setting his mug down on the small table between them. "I've seen men like Kevin before. They come in, make a mess of things, and leave the people picking up the pieces. But you're doing the right thing, son. Standing up to him."

Luke exhaled, rubbing the back of his neck. "It's more than just the town, though. I've got... personal reasons for staying now."

His dad raised an eyebrow, a slight smile tugging at the corners of his mouth. "Personal reasons, huh? I think I know what—or who—that might be."

Luke chuckled, though his tone was serious. "Emma. I've always had feelings for her, but now... it's stronger than ever. I want to be there for her, and for this town. But with everything going on, I'm not sure if I'm doing enough."

His dad sat up straighter, looking at him with a mix of pride and something deeper. "You've become a man I'm proud of, Luke. You're doing more than enough. Protecting this town, looking out for Emma... that's a lot on your shoulders. But you've handled it well."

Luke glanced at his dad, surprised by the weight of his words. "I just want to make sure I'm doing the right thing."

"You are," his dad said firmly. "And I'm glad you're back. Carter's Creek needs men like you, but more than that... I need you. I've missed having you around. I hope you're planning to stick around longer than just this fight."

Luke felt the tug of emotion, the kind that had always been harder to express. "I am. I don't plan on leaving again."

His dad smiled, the kind of smile that said more than words. "Good. We need each other, you and me. And maybe... you and Emma need each other too."

Luke let out a breath, feeling the weight of his dad's support settle over him. It wasn't just about protecting the town anymore—it was about staying, building something lasting. Something real.

***

FAMILY TIES AND SEEKING TRUTH

Emma sat at her desk, a notebook open in front of her, scribbling down notes as she made call after call to officials in neighboring towns. She had already spoken to two people who had worked directly with Kevin and had shared unsettling stories about the lengths he went to in order to secure his development deals.

"Yeah, we had a similar situation over in Riverside Heights," a city planner from a neighboring town was saying over the phone. "He promised jobs, improvements, the whole nine yards. But once he got his approvals, he cut corners everywhere. He fast-tracked permits and leaned on council members until they gave in."

Emma's stomach turned as she wrote down every word. "And did it benefit the town?"

"Not in the long run. He left before the final stages, moved on to his next project. We were stuck cleaning up the mess."

She thanked the official and ended the call, sitting back in her chair, her mind buzzing with worry. Kevin was nothing if not consistent—his pattern was clear, and it was the same one he was trying to pull in Carter's Creek.

Just as she reached for the phone to make another call, the sound of the front door opening pulled her attention away. Her mother appeared in the doorway, smiling brightly, holding a beautiful bouquet of flowers freshly picked from the church parsonage garden. Her dad was trailing behind, looking slightly uncomfortable as he followed her in.

"Thought I'd bring you a little something to brighten your day," her mom said, setting the bouquet on Emma's desk. "You've been working too hard."

Emma smiled softly, appreciating the gesture but already sensing the real reason for their visit. "Thanks, Mom. They're beautiful."

Her mom lingered, glancing at her husband before casually leaning against the desk. "So... I've noticed Luke's been around quite a bit lately. Seems like the two of you have been spending some time together."

Emma's face flushed slightly as she tucked a strand of hair behind her ear. "We're just working on town stuff, Mom. There's a lot going on with Kevin and the council. Nothing more to it."

Her mom's eyes sparkled knowingly. "Mmhmm. I wasn't born yesterday, Emma. It's not just town business, is it? Luke seems... different this time. More settled."

Emma opened her mouth to respond, but her dad jumped in. "Mind your own business, dear," he said gently but firmly, giving Emma a small nod of understanding. "Emma's got enough on her plate without us meddling in her personal life."

Her mom gave him a playful nudge. "I'm just saying, it seems like something's blooming there. And I'm all for it."

Emma couldn't help but chuckle, though her heart raced at the thought. "Mom, seriously, we're focused on protecting the town right now. That's all."

Her mom smiled, undeterred. "Well, just know I approve. He's a good one."

Her dad sighed, taking her mom by the arm and steering her toward the door. "Come on now, let's let Emma get back to work."

As they left, Emma found herself staring at the bouquet, her mind wandering. Was her mom right? Was there more between her and Luke? The idea of a future with him wasn't as distant as it once felt. She could almost picture it, but the reality of Kevin's looming threat crashed back in.

This problem with Kevin had to be solved first. Shaking off the thoughts, she refocused, organizing the notes from her calls and

FAMILY TIES AND SEEKING TRUTH   79

building the file of evidence against Kevin. It wasn't time for romance just yet—there was still too much at stake.

***

Gabe and Sadie approached the town hall with a shared look of determination. In a town like Carter's Creek, everyone knew everyone, and this was both an advantage and a challenge. Sadie knew the receptionist well—Mrs. Alice, who had been working in the permits office since she could remember. And Mrs. Alice, of course, knew all about Gabe, the town's newest bartender with a growing reputation.

"Let's keep this friendly," Sadie whispered as they stepped inside.

The familiar bell above the door chimed, and Mrs. Alice looked up from her desk with a warm but slightly strained smile. "Sadie! Gabe! What brings you two to the office today?"

Sadie leaned on the counter, offering a casual smile. "Hey, Mrs. Alice. We're just checking on a few details for Founder's Day. You know how it is—last-minute organizing, making sure everything's set. Thought we'd see how the permit approvals are coming along."

Mrs. Alice's smile faltered just slightly, though she quickly recovered. "Oh, well, you know, it's been busier than usual around here. A lot of projects moving through. Kevin Daniels has got half the town stirred up with his developments."

Gabe, watching the exchange, leaned in. "Seems like things are getting pushed through fast. We're just trying to make sure everything's going by the book."

Mrs. Alice shifted uncomfortably, her hands folding the edge of a piece of paper. "Well, you know how it is in a small town, Gabe. Things can move a little... quicker when certain folks are involved."

Sadie's voice softened, her eyes studying Mrs. Alice's nervous fidgeting. "Alice, you know me. I'm not here to cause trouble. But people are talking, and it's got me worried. It's not just about Founder's Day. Kevin's pushing things faster than normal, isn't he?"

Mrs. Alice's gaze darted around the room, making sure no one else was within earshot. She sighed, leaning in as if to confide. "Sadie, you didn't hear this from me, but yes. Kevin's projects... they're moving faster than I've ever seen. The council's got their hands all over it, pushing things through without the usual reviews."

Gabe exchanged a knowing look with Sadie. "And the council? Who's the one pushing hardest for Kevin?"

Mrs. Alice hesitated, lowering her voice even more. "You'd have to talk to Councilman Jenkins. He's been in a lot of closed-door meetings with Kevin lately. The rest of the council doesn't seem to be asking questions—at least, not publicly."

Sadie frowned. "Why are they doing this? What's the rush?"

Mrs. Alice's shoulders slumped slightly. "There's pressure. I don't know from where, but I can tell you—some of these council members are benefiting from it. They've got something to gain. And Kevin's not the type to leave loose ends."

Sadie nodded. "Thanks, Mrs. Alice. I know this wasn't easy."

Mrs. Alice gave her a tight smile. "Just be careful, Sadie. You and Gabe both. Kevin's got eyes everywhere."

As they left the office, Gabe shook his head. "Jenkins and the council, huh? This goes deeper than we thought."

Sadie agreed. "And it's happening fast. We've got to get more solid proof before Kevin locks down his approvals. Let's see what else we can dig up."

***

FAMILY TIES AND SEEKING TRUTH 81

Emma's loft above the bakery was a familiar haven, but tonight it felt heavier, filled with tension and unanswered questions. The group had gathered—Sadie, Gabe, Tommy, and Hannah—waiting for Luke, who had yet to show. Emma glanced at her phone, frustration edging into her expression.

"No word from Luke?" Sadie asked, sensing Emma's growing unease.

Emma shook her head, setting her phone down on the table. "Nothing. I've called him a few times. He knew we were meeting tonight."

Hannah leaned forward, her voice tinged with concern. "Do you think something happened? This isn't like him."

Emma sighed but forced herself to focus. "I don't know. Maybe he's just caught up in something. But we can't wait for him to start. We've got to keep moving."

Just then, the door opened, and Luke finally walked in. He looked slightly disheveled, his usual easygoing demeanor a little off, though he attempted a casual smile. "Sorry I'm late. Got tied up."

The group exchanged glances, but Emma, still relieved to see him, motioned for him to sit. "We were worried. Where've you been?"

Luke shrugged, avoiding her gaze. "Just dealing with a few things. Nothing to worry about."

Emma's eyes lingered on him, the tension clear, but she decided to focus on the task at hand. "Alright, let's get started. We need to figure out what Kevin's up to and how to stop him."

She took a breath and turned to the group, starting her report. "I've been calling town officials in Riverside Heights, Briarwood Estates, and Silver Creek Development. They're still cleaning up after Kevin's projects, but the thing is—Kevin walked away profitable, leaving everyone else to deal with the fallout. He fast-tracks the permits, cuts corners, and leaves behind half-finished developments. The towns are left in chaos, but Kevin pockets the profits and moves on to the next one."

Gabe frowned, leaning back in his chair. "So he's leaving towns to pick up the pieces while he lines his pockets?"

Emma nodded. "Exactly. And that's what he's trying to do here. If we don't find a way to stop him, Carter's Creek will be his next victim."

Sadie spoke next, her tone serious. "We visited Mrs. Alice at the permits office. She's scared but admitted that Kevin's projects are moving faster than anything she's ever seen. And it's all being pushed through by Councilman Jenkins. He's working with Kevin, meeting privately and cutting through the red tape."

Gabe added, "Mrs. Alice hinted that Jenkins isn't the only one benefitting from this. There's pressure from somewhere—Kevin's investors, maybe—but Jenkins is at the center of it. He's making sure Kevin's deals go through fast."

Emma's jaw tightened as she scribbled notes. "If we can prove Jenkins is personally gaining from this, we might have a way to stop them. I'm sure Kevin's investors are pushing him, which is why he's rushing everything."

Luke, who had been silent, finally spoke. "I talked to my dad about this. He's seen men like Kevin come and go. He thinks some of the older council members might not even realize how deep Kevin's got them. But Jenkins? He's knowingly in Kevin's pocket, pushing everything through. My dad's worried if we don't move fast, Kevin will have all the approvals he needs."

The group fell quiet as they processed Luke's words. Emma took a deep breath, pulling herself back into the moment. "Alright. We need more evidence before we can act. Sadie, see if you can dig into Jenkins'

FAMILY TIES AND SEEKING TRUTH

connections. Gabe, listen around the tavern. Someone's bound to slip up and talk."

The team nodded in agreement, ready to move forward. But even as the conversation shifted back to Kevin, the tension between Luke and Emma was hard to ignore.

After the meeting ended, Luke and Tommy stepped outside, huddling near the door. "You good, man?" Tommy asked, his tone low and concerned.

Luke glanced over his shoulder toward the loft, making sure they weren't overheard. "Yeah. Just a lot on my plate."

Tommy eyed him. "Emma's worried about you. You should probably talk to her."

Luke exhaled, rubbing the back of his neck. "I will. Just... not yet. There's too much going on."

Meanwhile, inside the loft, Emma sat on the couch with Hannah, her concern clear. "You've noticed how off Luke's been, right?"

Hannah nodded. "Yeah, he's definitely not himself. Do you think it's something to do with Kevin?"

Emma frowned, unsure. "I don't know. But something's going on, and I'm starting to worry he's hiding something from me."

Hannah gave her a reassuring squeeze on the arm. "Whatever it is, we'll figure it out. Luke's always had your back."

Emma smiled faintly, but the nagging feeling in her chest didn't disappear. Something wasn't adding up, and she wasn't sure how long she could ignore it.

Chapter Ten
Secrets & Strategies

The small office was filled with the sound of rustling papers as Emma, Sadie, and Hannah worked through their research. Documents and old records were spread across the table, each more damning than the last.

"Okay, so we've established that Jenkins was in the same fraternity at State U as some of Kevin's investors," Emma said, tapping a highlighted section on a printed sheet.

Sadie flipped through her notes, her brow furrowed. "Right, but it's more than that. Look here." She passed Emma a list of names, some familiar, some not. "These guys weren't just frat brothers. Jenkins has cousins and close fraternity brothers in towns where Kevin pushed through his past projects. I found the cousins connected to him on social media."

Emma's eyes widened as she scanned the names, and then she stopped abruptly. "Wait a minute. I know this name." She pointed to one in the middle of the list. "Charles Dixon. My dad went to school with him."

Hannah, leaning against the door, straightened up. "Seriously? Small world."

Emma nodded, a slight frown crossing her face. "Yeah, but I didn't realize he was connected to Jenkins. If Charles is involved in those projects, there's a good chance Jenkins has been helping Kevin through more than just financial ties. He's probably leveraging personal relationships. I always thought of Charles as a straight arrow."

Sadie leaned in, her curiosity piqued. "So Jenkins isn't just fast-tracking Kevin's permits because of the investors. He's got family and close friends benefiting from this too."

Hannah crossed her arms, thoughtful. "And if these guys are still meeting regularly, they're probably sharing more than just college memories. They're coordinating."

Emma leaned back in her chair, her mind racing. "Their next meeting is this weekend, right?"

Sadie nodded. "Yeah. Twice a year. Once with the whole frat house, and once with this smaller group—mostly the ones tied to these deals."

Emma's eyes narrowed. "We need to figure out how to use this. If Jenkins and his connections are this deep, we need to know what's being said at that meeting."

Hannah raised an eyebrow. "Think your dad would know anything more about Charles Dixon?"

Emma shrugged. "Maybe. I'll ask, but for now, let's plan to find a way to get more information. This weekend is our chance."

***

The late afternoon sun streamed through the large front windows of the tavern, casting long shadows across the wooden floors. It was a slower time before happy hour, so Gabe leaned against the bar, restocking clean glasses and cleaning up after the lunch rush, enjoying the calm.

Just then, Ms. Beatrice and Mabel, two of the town's most avid gossips, made their way in. They were regulars, known for their penchant for Shirley Temples and their love of a good story. Today, they decided to grab a table by the front window, giving them a clear view of both the bustling street outside and the happenings inside the tavern.

"Gabe, darling, can we get two of your finest Shirley Temples?" Ms. Beatrice asked, her eyes twinkling with excitement.

"Coming right up," Gabe replied with a warm smile. "You two look like you've got something on your minds."

As he prepared their drinks, Mabel leaned closer, her voice dropping to a conspiratorial whisper. "Have you heard about Councilman Jenkins lately?"

Gabe raised an eyebrow, intrigued. "Can't say I have. What's he up to?"

Ms. Beatrice giggled, placing her hands gracefully on the bar. "Oh, you know Jenkins. Always been a bit of a schemer. Well, it turns out he's been coming into some serious money recently."

Gabe's interest was piqued. "Really? Any idea where it's coming from?"

Mabel shrugged, sipping her drink thoughtfully. "Rumor has it his secretary was sharing about some lucrative deals they've got cooking. I'm never sure about anything she says though."

Ms. Beatrice nodded enthusiastically. "Absolutely! And there's more—people are whispering that someone's been missing around town. Might just be a tourist passing through, but that's not normal for Carter's Creek."

Gabe frowned slightly, processing the information. "Missing? That's concerning. Have you heard anything more concrete?"

Mabel shook her head, a worried look crossing her face. "Nothing solid. Just a lot of talk and speculation. But with Jenkins pulling in all that money, it makes you wonder if there's more to it."

Ms. Beatrice glanced out the window, her expression thoughtful. "It's just not like the quiet town we know anymore. There's so much happening, and not all of it good."

Gabe leaned in, lowering his voice. "If someone's missing, we need to keep an eye out. I'll make sure to stay alert and see if I can gather any more information."

Mabel smiled reassuringly. "We all are, dear. It's just hard not knowing what's going on. But knowing you're looking out for everyone gives us some peace of mind."

As the two women continued their conversation, Gabe couldn't shake the feeling that there was more beneath the surface. Jenkins' newfound wealth and the rumors of a missing person hinted at deeper troubles in Carter's Creek. He made a mental note to keep a closer watch on Jenkins and the town's activities, especially with the upcoming fraternity meeting that could shed more light on the councilman's dealings.

As Ms. Beatrice and Mabel left to join their table by the window, Gabe returned to his tasks, his mind racing with the new gossip. That's when he realized Linda hadn't been back in since her run-in with Kevin a couple of days ago. He picked up the phone to call her, but the calls all went to voicemail.

The pieces were starting to fall into place, but he knew he needed to tread carefully. Protecting the town meant uncovering the truth—and making sure Linda was okay—no matter how tangled the web became.

***

The sun cast a warm glow through the large windows of the town hall meeting room, illuminating the dust particles that danced in the air. Emma stood at the front of the long wooden table, shuffling her notes and trying to ignore the empty chair where Luke was supposed to be. His absence gnawed at her, adding to the weight of responsibilities already pressing on her shoulders.

"Thank you all for coming," Emma began, forcing a confident smile as she addressed the committee members seated around the table. "We have a lot to cover today to ensure Founder's Day is a success."

The committee dove into discussions about parade routes, vendor placements, and entertainment schedules. Emma guided the conversation, her leadership steady despite the undercurrent of anxiety she felt. As the meeting progressed, she caught Councilman Jenkins watching her with a calculated gaze.

When a brief recess was called, Jenkins approached her, his polished shoes clicking softly against the hardwood floor.

"Mayor Thompson," he said smoothly, adjusting his tie. "A word, if you don't mind."

Emma turned to face him, maintaining a neutral expression. "Of course, Councilman Jenkins. How can I help you?"

He smiled, but it didn't reach his eyes. "I've been hearing some concerns around town about the preparations for Founder's Day. Some feel that perhaps more experienced leadership could ensure everything runs smoothly."

Emma felt a flicker of irritation but kept her tone even. "I appreciate the feedback, but the committee and I have everything well in hand. We've successfully managed this event for the past several years."

Jenkins tilted his head slightly. "Still, with all the... distractions lately, one might worry about where your focus lies."

She knew he was baiting her, perhaps hoping she'd react impulsively. But now wasn't the time to push back; she needed to choose her battles carefully.

"Founder's Day is a priority for me," Emma replied calmly. "I assure you, nothing will interfere with its success."

He raised an eyebrow, clearly expecting more of a reaction. "Glad to hear it. If you need any assistance, don't hesitate to reach out. After all, we all want what's best for Carter's Creek."

"Thank you for your concern," she said, offering a polite smile. "I'll keep that in mind."

Jenkins lingered for a moment before nodding and walking away, his footsteps fading as he exited the room. Emma released a quiet sigh, her gaze drifting back to the empty chair. She couldn't help but wish Luke were there; his support always steadied her nerves during interactions like this.

The committee members began to reconvene, and Emma straightened her shoulders, pushing aside her frustrations. There would be a better time to address Jenkins and his undermining comments. For now, she had a meeting to lead and an event to plan.

"Alright, everyone," she announced, projecting confidence. "Let's get back to it. We still need to finalize the schedule for the day."

As the discussions resumed, Emma focused on the task at hand. She knew that standing firm was the best way to counter any doubts about her leadership—even if she had to do it without Luke by her side.

***

The evening air was crisp as Emma, Sadie, and Hannah left Town Hall, their steps echoing softly on the quiet street. Each of them was wrapped in their own thoughts, minds racing with the revelations about Jenkins' fraternity ties and the increasing web of threats facing the town. Emma couldn't shake the weight of it all, but her thoughts kept circling back to something else—or rather, someone.

Luke hadn't been at the meeting, and for the first time all day, it struck her just how absent he'd been. From the bakery to the tavern, she'd looked for him in each place they'd stopped, hoping to catch a glimpse of him. It was unlike him to disappear when things were heating up, and his absence left her feeling unmoored, facing a darkness she wasn't sure she could navigate alone.

Inside the tavern, the usual hum of voices surrounded them, familiar yet slightly off, as though everyone sensed something amiss. Gabe was behind the bar, polishing glasses with a thoughtful frown as they approached.

Sadie slid onto a barstool, nodding at Gabe. "Anything new?"

Gabe's expression turned grim as he set the glass down and leaned closer. "Nothing good. The girls were in earlier with their usual gossip, but there's real talk this time. Councilman Jenkins' secretary says he's got some 'lucrative deals in the works.' And, bigger still, they've heard that someone's gone missing, but they're not sure who. And that's when it hit me—Linda hasn't been around since that run-in with Kevin. I've tried calling her, but no luck."

Emma's worry spiked. "Do we know for sure it's her?"

Gabe nodded, looking troubled. "It's official now. One of the deputies stopped by with a missing persons poster, asked me to put it up. She's been missing since the night before last."

Hannah's hand flew to her mouth, her face paling. "Linda? Missing? This is definitely connected to Kevin—she knows too much, especially after what she saw him push through at the council meeting."

Emma took a steadying breath, feeling the familiar weight of responsibility press on her. "We can't just wait for news. If she's hiding, we need to help her. And if she's been taken..." Her voice trailed off, unable to finish the thought. "We need to know where she went last."

Sadie tapped her fingers thoughtfully on the bar. "You're right. We should start by retracing her steps, see if anyone saw something she didn't tell us." Then, after a pause, she added, "You know, losing that election and then his wife... it changed him. I think Jenkins truly believed he was next in line to run the town, and when that didn't happen, he was never the same."

Emma glanced at Sadie, absorbing her words. "So it's not just business with him," she murmured. "It's personal."

Sadie nodded, her expression grim. "Exactly. I think he's doing this partly out of resentment, and Kevin's taking full advantage of that."

Before anyone could respond, the tavern door swung open, and Tommy stepped in, his face shadowed with worry. He joined them, taking in the expressions on each of their faces before speaking.

"Hey. Heard about Linda?" His voice was quiet, laced with concern. "If Kevin's got anything to do with this, we need to find her fast."

Emma offered a reassuring smile, though her mind was racing. "We're already on it, Tommy. We just need to be careful."

After a few more minutes of planning, they each set off with tasks for the morning. Emma and Sadie were the last to leave, and as they stepped out into the night, Emma felt the chill settle deeper than usual. The urgency of Linda's disappearance weighed on her, and yet, her mind drifted to Luke. She hadn't seen him all day—not a glimpse or even a message. And the more she thought about it, the more the uncertainty gnawed at her.

Later, Emma sat alone in her loft, wrapped in a blanket as she stared out the window into the quiet night. Normally, she would've had

Luke by her side, helping her talk through the endless details of the day. But tonight, it was just her and the growing silence. She glanced over at a photo on her shelf, one of her and Luke laughing together, and a pang of longing washed over her. His absence left an ache she wasn't sure how to fill.

With a sigh, she grabbed her phone, hesitating briefly before typing out a message: *Hey Luke, I need to talk to you urgently. Linda is missing, and we really need your help. Can you come over tonight?*

Seconds ticked by, and she felt her anxiety deepen with each one. Why hadn't he been anywhere in town today? Had she done something, or was he facing something he hadn't shared with her? Finally, her phone buzzed with a reply, pulling her from her thoughts.

Just saw your message. I'm on my way. Stay strong. I'll be right there.

She exhaled, relief flooding over her, though her mind was still buzzing with questions. She could feel the weight of the day pressing down on her, and though she was grateful he'd replied, his recent absences left her feeling uncertain. At least, she thought with a small measure of comfort, he was still a call away—even if it felt like he'd drifted somewhere she couldn't quite reach.

And as she set her phone down, preparing herself for the conversation ahead, she couldn't shake the feeling that Luke's presence, though reassuring, brought just as many questions as answers.

Chapter Eleven
Showdowns & Unexpected Alliances

THE GENTLE SOUNDS OF the night drifted through the open windows of Emma's loft, mingling with the aroma of freshly brewed coffee from the kitchen. Emma sat at her cluttered dining table, surrounded by scattered papers and notes, a silent testament to the day's discoveries and the heavy task of piecing everything together. Her phone lay on the table beside her, the recent text to Luke a silent thread of hope amid her worry:

Hey Luke, I need to talk to you urgently. Linda is missing, and we really need your help. Can you come over tonight?

When the quiet knock finally came, she felt a flood of relief mixed with a pang of tension. She took a steadying breath and went to the door, opening it to find Luke standing there, his eyes full of concern, though his expression was tired, as if he carried his own unseen burdens.

"Hey, Emma," he said softly, stepping inside and closing the door behind him. "I'm sorry I wasn't around today. What's going on?"

Emma motioned for him to sit, her hands slightly shaky as she collected herself. "Thank you for coming so quickly," she began, her voice steady but carrying the day's weight. "It's... it's a lot."

Luke sat, his gaze never leaving hers, and for a moment, the familiar warmth in his eyes reassured her. Emma took a breath and plunged in. "We discovered today that Jenkins and some of his investors—turns out they were fraternity brothers at State U. They're having a meeting this weekend, and it could be our best shot to learn more about his connections to Kevin's projects."

Luke nodded slowly, his focus sharpening. "That's serious. And the timing... It feels like everything's about to come to a head."

Emma's voice grew quieter, more vulnerable. "And, now Linda's missing! I've tried calling her, but her phone goes straight to voicemail. And she's not the type to leave without saying something," she added, worry evident in her tone. "She was just heading home from the tavern that night. I can't imagine why she'd go off without a word."

She looked at him, her expression a mixture of frustration and worry. "Then there's you, Luke. You've been helping me through all this, and suddenly, nowhere to be found. What's going on? Can I still count on you?"

Luke exhaled deeply, running a hand through his hair as he settled back in his chair, his expression softened by her words. "I know I haven't been around, Emma, and I'm sorry for that," he said, his tone sincere. "There's been a lot I needed to work through, and I didn't want to drag you into it. But I promise, I'm here now."

Emma crossed her arms, her gaze searching his face. "You're here now, but I need more than that. Linda's life could be at stake. We've all been counting on you, and I need to know you won't just disappear."

Luke leaned forward, his tone low and earnest. "I'm not going anywhere. Whatever's going on with Linda, whatever's happening with Jenkins and his investors—we're going to figure this out together. I had reasons for stepping away, but I won't let you down."

Emma held his gaze for a long moment, letting his words sink in, searching his face for any sign of doubt. Finally, she nodded, her voice soft but firm. "Alright. But I need you all in. No more secrets, no more vanishing acts."

He nodded, his eyes full of quiet resolve. "You have my word."

She handed him a folder, her fingers brushing his as she pointed out the latest documents. "Take a look at this. Jenkins has been funneling money into accounts connected to Kevin's project, and it's all under layers of shell companies. It's all too carefully hidden, but we're close to connecting the dots. And now, with Linda missing... it feels like it's all part of the same puzzle."

Luke's brow furrowed as he flipped through the pages, his expression darkening. "This is bigger than I thought. Jenkins isn't going to back down, not with this much at stake. But that doesn't mean he can just walk all over us."

Emma sighed, her worry showing in the tension around her eyes. "Exactly. And the stakes just got even higher now that someone's missing. We can't let them get away with this."

A heavy silence settled between them, the weight of their mission pressing down like an invisible force. Luke finally broke the stillness, his tone decisive. "We need to gather more information before this weekend. I'll dig around, see what I can find. You should ask around town, see if anyone has any leads on Linda."

Emma nodded, feeling a mix of relief and weariness. For the first time that day, she didn't feel completely alone in this. "Let's split up, cover as much ground as possible before Friday."

There was a pause as they both stood, his presence grounding her in a way she hadn't realized she'd missed. She felt the stress of the day's events start to recede, if only slightly, as they prepared to part ways. And then, just as Luke turned to reach for the door, he hesitated, glancing back.

In a rare moment of vulnerability, he took a step toward her and wrapped her in a hug, his arms encircling her shoulders. She stiffened for a second, but then melted into his embrace, gripping the back of his shirt as if holding onto something solid in the midst of the chaos.

Luke pressed a gentle kiss to the top of her head, his lips lingering just a heartbeat longer than expected. "We're going to figure this out," he whispered softly, his voice a quiet promise.

Emma didn't reply, only held onto him, letting the moment speak for itself. For just a second, the troubles of the town faded, and she allowed herself to find comfort in the warmth of his arms, in the familiar scent of him that felt like coming home.

As he pulled back, his hands lingered on her arms, giving them a gentle squeeze. "We've got this. I'll keep you posted on what I find."

Emma nodded, her heart settling as she watched him leave, still feeling the warmth of his embrace. For the first time in days, despite the weight of their mission, she felt a glimmer of hope. Whatever they were about to face, she wouldn't be facing it alone.

***

The grand oak doors of the town hall swung open, inviting the evening's attendees into the vaulted meeting room. The soft murmur of town council members, local business owners, and concerned citizens filled the space, all gathered to discuss the upcoming Founder's Day festivities—and, unspoken but palpable, the recent controversies surrounding Councilman Jenkins.

Emma stood at the front, her posture straight and eyes focused, exuding a calm she didn't entirely feel. She had meticulously prepared for this meeting, knowing the revelations about Jenkins' connections could no longer remain in the shadows. Her phone buzzed silently in her pocket—a message from Luke confirming he was on his way, though running a bit late. She cast a glance around the room, noticing her father seated on one side, while Luke's father sat on the opposite. Why couldn't they just find some common ground and get along, she wondered.

As the meeting commenced, the agenda moved smoothly from parade routes to vendor arrangements. However, a simmering tension lay just beneath the surface, especially with Jenkins seated directly across from Emma, his demeanor cool and composed. Too composed.

After several agenda items were addressed, Emma took a deep breath, feeling the weight of the room's expectations. This was her moment. She couldn't delay any longer. The fast-tracked permits for Kevin's development projects had to be addressed.

"Council members, esteemed guests," Emma began, her voice steady but charged with determination. "I'd like to raise some concerns regarding the recent permits approved for Kevin Daniels' projects."

A ripple of murmurs spread through the crowd. Eyes shifted toward Jenkins, who remained disturbingly calm, his expression betraying nothing.

Emma clicked her remote, and a projector screen illuminated behind her, displaying the detailed report she had compiled. "As many of you know, Kevin Pollard has apparently began several development projects in Carter's Creek. While development is crucial for our town's growth, the speed at which these permits have been approved raises significant concerns."

She advanced to the next slide, showcasing financial records and correspondence linking Jenkins to key investors in Kevin's ventures. "It has come to my attention that Councilman Jenkins, along with several other council members, have longstanding ties with Kevin's investors—ties that date back to their fraternity days at State U."

The room fell silent, tension thickening the air as Emma's words settled. Jenkins leaned forward, his expression still unreadable. "Emma, these are serious allegations. Do you have concrete evidence, or are you basing this on old associations?"

Emma held his gaze. "Yes, Councilman Jenkins. Not only do these ties exist, but they appear to be the driving force behind the expedited approval of Kevin's permits. These are not the standard procedures we've adhered to in the past."

A flicker of irritation crossed Jenkins' face. "Expedited permits are sometimes necessary for the town's growth. If you have concerns about my integrity, maybe you should focus on your own role in the council, rather than on me."

Emma didn't flinch, her resolve only hardening. "My role, Councilman, is to ensure Carter's Creek operates with transparency. If these permits are being pushed through for personal gain, it's our duty to address it now."

Silence enveloped the room as Jenkins struggled to maintain his composure. His hands clenched tightly together in front of him, and he leaned back in his chair, exhaling slowly. "Emma, I assure you, all permits are being handled in the town's best interests. Your insistence on this matter is noted, but you may be overstepping your role as mayor."

Emma took a step forward, her voice firm. "Overstepping? Councilman Jenkins, this isn't about roles—it's about accountability. Carter's Creek deserves to know the truth behind these permits. Are we advancing our town's prosperity, or are we serving the interests of a few with hidden agendas?"

The crowd buzzed with murmurs of agreement, and Jenkins' gaze darted around the room, searching for support but finding little. His frustration was palpable.

Just then, the door creaked open, and Luke entered, slightly out of breath but resolute. His presence immediately shifted the room's energy, adding a much-needed layer of support for Emma. Jenkins' eyes narrowed as he glanced at Luke, a mix of frustration and calculation in his gaze.

"Luke," Jenkins snapped, "you don't have a dog in this hunt. Why are you even here? Perhaps you should leave before you embarrass yourself—or the mayor."

Luke ignored the jab, stepping beside Emma without hesitation. His presence was enough to bolster her resolve. She squared her shoulders and faced Jenkins again, unwavering.

"No, Councilman," she said, her voice cutting through the tension. "The truth doesn't embarrass me. Carter's Creek deserves transparency, and I intend to provide it."

Jenkins' jaw tightened, but before he could respond, Emma turned to the room, her voice ringing with authority. "I propose we move forward with an official investigation into these permits. It's the only way to ensure that our town remains honest and fair for everyone. All in favor, raise your hands," Emma paused, then continued, "All opposed, by the same sign."

The room erupted in a mix of whispers and murmurs as Emma's bold confrontation settled over the assembly. The vote was very telling. Every member of the council voted in favor of an investigation, with the only vote opposing it was Jenkins himself. Jenkins clenched his fists under the table, realizing his carefully constructed facade was beginning to crumble, and he knew who to blame.

As the meeting pressed on, the seeds of conflict had been firmly planted. Emma's stand had not only challenged Jenkins' integrity but had also rallied those in the room who believed in transparency and ethical governance. The fight for Carter's Creek had just begun.

***

Jenkins stormed into Kevin's office, his expression etched with frustration. He didn't bother with pleasantries or formalities; he simply shut the door and glared across the room. "We need to talk, now."

Kevin looked up leisurely, a smirk already dancing on his lips. He didn't seem the least bit surprised by Jenkins' arrival. "What's on your mind, Jenkins? I'm sure it's something important if you came all the way down here in the middle of the night."

Jenkins didn't sit. Instead, he gripped the back of a chair in front of Kevin's desk, his knuckles white with barely controlled anger. "You assured me there'd be no risks," he hissed. "Smooth as silk, you said. Now I've got the council opening an investigation into my actions on the permits for your project. And, as if that weren't enough, Linda's gone missing. No one's seen her in days, Kevin."

Kevin leaned back, his smirk unwavering. "Linda? Really, Jenkins, I thought you were more level-headed. She's probably just off on a little trip—taking some personal time, maybe? Happens all the time, right?"

Jenkins' frown deepened, his frustration morphing into something close to fear. "Linda doesn't just disappear without telling someone.

People are starting to talk, and they're starting to look at me, Kevin. If something's happened to her—if she's been hurt, or worse..."

Kevin finally stood, moving around his desk with a slow, calculated stride, his expression growing colder. "Relax, Jenkins. You're getting worked up over nothing. Linda's a grown woman—she can take care of herself."

Jenkins' eyes narrowed, suspicion creeping in. "You seem awfully confident, Kevin. Almost like... you know something the rest of us don't. Do you have anything to tell me?"

Kevin chuckled, a dark, humorless sound. "I told you to keep your head down and let me handle things. That's what you're being paid for, remember? Handsomely, I might add."

Jenkins shifted uncomfortably, his nerves starting to fray. "I didn't sign up for people disappearing, Kevin. I was under the impression we were handling this above board—within reason, anyway. If you're dragging us into something beyond that..."

Kevin's gaze hardened, cutting him off. "It's under control. All you have to do is hold your ground, keep quiet, and stay out of my way. You can do that, can't you?"

Jenkins' face flushed with anger, but his voice was laced with reluctant resignation as he turned to leave. "Just remember, if this backfires, I'm not going down alone."

Kevin watched him go, a faint smile touching his lips as Jenkins disappeared out the door. Still stirred up from the confrontation, Kevin decided a walk might help clear his head. He slipped on his coat, heading out of his office and into the cool night air. The town square was quiet, the streetlights casting long shadows as he made his way toward the gazebo. That's when he spotted Luke and Emma standing near the structure, their heads close as they discussed something quietly.

Kevin's smirk returned, and he approached them with a practiced charm. "Emma! Always a pleasure," he greeted smoothly, his eyes lingering on her a second too long. "The gazebo's looking good, Luke. What's a handsome couple like you doing out here at this time of night?"

Emma stiffened, her eyes narrowing. She stepped forward, her voice calm but firm. "Kevin, you should know—the council's starting an investigation into those permits you pushed through. Questions are being asked, and you're right at the center of it."

Kevin's jaw tightened, but he kept his voice smooth. "The council? Investigating me? After all I've done for this town?" He let out a low laugh, feigning disbelief. "Sounds like a waste of time. I've got nothing to hide."

Luke, arms crossed, stepped closer, his gaze hard and unyielding. "You might want to think that through, Kevin. The sheriff's getting involved too—especially since you were seen arguing with Linda right before she disappeared."

Kevin's expression faltered for just a moment, his charm slipping to reveal a cold, calculating edge. "Linda?" he repeated, his tone dismissive. "There was nothing serious there. Just a little... companionship. I'd suggest, Luke, that you don't start digging into things that don't concern you. People who stir the pot tend to get burned."

Emma's gaze sharpened, her voice filled with barely controlled anger. "Is that a threat, Kevin?"

Kevin met her gaze with a smile that didn't reach his eyes. "Not at all, Emma. Just a bit of friendly advice. Stick to what you know best. Developments like mine might be a little above your pay grade." Then, turning his attention to Luke, he added, "Funny, isn't it, Luke? All those years you were the golden boy, always in the spotlight, while the rest of us were in the shadows. Now look at you—and look at me. I'm the one calling the shots."

Luke took a step forward, his fists clenched, a spark of anger flashing in his eyes, but Emma quickly put a hand on his arm, grounding him. Kevin watched the exchange with a bemused smile, his eyes glinting with satisfaction.

"I'm just looking out for the bigger picture, Emma," Kevin continued smoothly. "Push too hard, and you might find yourself on the outside of Carter's Creek. Wouldn't that be a shame?"

Emma held her ground, her expression fierce, but before she could respond, Kevin gave a casual shrug and turned on his heel, walking away without another word. The night air felt colder in the silence he left behind.

As he disappeared down the street, Emma released a breath she hadn't realized she was holding, her hand still resting on Luke's arm. She looked up at him, her eyes full of a mixture of frustration and determination. "This isn't over. He's hiding something, and we're going to find out what it is."

Luke's jaw remained tight, his anger simmering just beneath the surface. "He's got something up his sleeve, Emma. And whatever it is, we're not letting him get away with it."

Together, they turned back toward the gazebo, the encounter with Kevin still hanging heavily in the air. Whatever the cost, they were ready to face it—together.

***

Before Emma or Luke could speak, two familiar figures stepped out of the shadows, their expressions surprisingly united. It was Emma's dad,

Pastor Thompson, and Luke's dad, Tom Hunter, walking side by side with a shared sense of purpose.

"Well, well. Looks like we missed the action," Pastor Thompson remarked, casting a glance down the road where Kevin had stormed off. His tone was light, but there was a steely glint in his eyes that betrayed his thoughts.

Tom nodded, his gaze following the same path. "Yeah, we saw that snake slither off."

Emma blinked, struggling to process the sight before her. "Dad? What are you two doing here—together?"

Luke raised an eyebrow, still not quite believing it himself. "This is... unexpected."

Pastor Thompson smirked. "It is, isn't it? But as it happens, your father and I had a little chat after the council meeting. Turns out we have some shared concerns about the way things are being handled—and the way Kevin's been pushing these permits through."

Tom crossed his arms, his expression more serious than usual. "We don't agree on much, but we do agree that Kevin's up to no good. And we figure the best way to handle this is to keep a close eye on things together."

Emma's eyes widened, still trying to wrap her head around the unlikely alliance. "So... you're working together?"

Tom shrugged, glancing sideways at Pastor Thompson. "Desperate times, desperate measures. Kevin's trying to turn this town upside down, and we don't plan on letting him get away with it."

Pastor Thompson nodded in agreement. "Exactly. The council may be handling the official investigation, but with both of us watching, we can make sure nothing gets overlooked. We won't let Kevin steamroll Carter's Creek."

Luke exchanged a bewildered look with Emma, both of them taken aback by the sudden show of unity. He turned to his father, still processing the sight of the two men standing side by side.

"You're both really on board with this?" Luke asked, his tone skeptical but hopeful.

Tom chuckled, shaking his head slightly. "Strange as it sounds, yes. We may not agree on a lot, but when it comes to protecting this town, we're on the same team."

Emma let out a small laugh, half in disbelief. "Wow. I honestly never thought I'd see the day."

Pastor Thompson smiled at her, resting a hand on her shoulder. "Don't get too used to it," he teased, though there was an underlying warmth in his voice. "But Kevin's trouble, and this town is more important than our differences. You two should be cautious—he's not the type to give up easily."

Tom nodded, his expression unusually serious as he looked at both Emma and Luke. "We'll handle the council side of things, and the sheriff will dig into Linda's disappearance. You two just focus on what you're good at. Keep your eyes open and don't let Kevin's tactics throw you off."

Emma glanced at Luke, a small smile tugging at her lips despite the tension. "I just want to protect this town."

Luke nodded, his jaw set with determination. "And we're not going to let Kevin tear it apart."

Pastor Thompson's gaze softened as he gave Emma's shoulder a reassuring squeeze. "And you don't have to do it alone, Emma. You've got more support than you realize. We're behind you every step of the way."

Tom gave a rare approving nod toward both Emma and Luke. "We've got your backs."

Luke looked from his father to Pastor Thompson, a look of quiet amazement in his eyes. "If you two are actually on the same side... maybe there's hope for Carter's Creek after all."

The two dads shared a small grin, their shared determination overriding years of stubborn differences. For a brief moment, the weight on Emma and Luke's shoulders felt a little lighter. There was a newfound sense of solidarity in the air—an unspoken understanding that, no matter how tough things got, they were all in this fight together.

Chapter Twelve
Fishing for Clues

THE STEADY HUM OF the road filled the cab, punctuating the silence between the two men. Tom Hunter's hands gripped the steering wheel a bit too tightly, his eyes fixed on the road ahead, while Daniel Thompson sat stiffly in the passenger seat, gazing out the window as the countryside passed by. The awkwardness was palpable, and neither seemed eager to break the silence.

It felt strange. As boys, they'd been inseparable, spending endless summers fishing, exploring the woods, and causing harmless mischief around Carter's Creek. They'd shared every secret, every ambition—until high school changed everything. Tom joined the popular crowd, became known as the guy with charm and a rebellious streak, while Daniel had focused on his studies, leaning into his faith and finding his calling in a different path. By graduation, they'd gone from best friends to near strangers, and the years had only widened the gap.

Now, here they were, decades later, on a road trip together in Tom's old truck, heading out to see Charles Dixon, an old friend of Daniel's who might have the information they needed to bring down Kevin Pollard's schemes. It was a mission for the town, and, more importantly, for their kids. But that didn't make it any less surreal.

Finally, Tom broke the silence, his voice rougher than usual. "How did we end up here, huh? On the road together in the same truck?"

Daniel shifted in his seat, a faint smile tugging at the corner of his mouth. "Good question," he replied, glancing over at Tom. "I suppose it was inevitable, though. Kevin's project isn't just some town scandal; it could change everything if we don't stop it. And if that means a little old-fashioned teamwork, well... here we are."

Tom let out a huff of a laugh, though his eyes stayed on the road. "Funny. Last time we were on a road trip together, we were sneaking off to the lake for one last fishing trip before school started. Now we're out here, trying to keep the town from turning into some... some development project."

Daniel chuckled, the sound tinged with nostalgia. "Yeah, and back then, we thought Carter's Creek was the whole world. Life's come full circle, hasn't it? And now here we are, heading to see Charles Dixon. I figured you'd want to hear what he has to say firsthand."

"Can't argue with that," Tom said, nodding. "I know he's your friend from college, and I know he'll talk to you. But Kevin's got his tentacles in everything. It'll be good to have another set of ears listening in."

Daniel nodded thoughtfully, gazing out at the open road. "Charles is a good man. His town's already faced off against Kevin's type of development, and they lost a lot to that project. I think he can help us piece together what we need to do before it's too late for Carter's Creek."

Tom considered this, the tension in his shoulders easing slightly. "I'll give him a fair listen. At this point, I'm open to any insight we can get." He shot a quick glance at Daniel. "But let's be honest—it's strange. You and me, working together again after all these years."

Daniel let out a small laugh, though there was an undercurrent of unease in his tone. "Strange, yeah. But I figure life's funny like that. Sometimes it throws us back together when we least expect it. Maybe it's a reminder that the past doesn't have to define the present."

Tom glanced over, his expression softening as he weighed Daniel's words. "Guess we weren't always on the same path back then. Maybe we still aren't. But... maybe we're not so different after all. We both want the same thing for this town."

They exchanged a brief look of understanding, a flicker of the friendship they'd once shared surfacing in the quiet of the truck cab. The years had changed them both, but, at least for now, they shared a common purpose. It felt like old times—different, but familiar enough to feel like home.

After a beat, Daniel cleared his throat, looking back out the window. "If we're going to do this, we do it right. No shortcuts. Kevin has connections, resources, and no problem using people to get what he wants. We'll have to stay one step ahead if we want to win."

Tom's grip on the wheel tightened again, his face hardening. "Agreed. I may not have the cleanest record, but when it comes to protecting Carter's Creek, I won't cut corners. And I won't let Kevin tear this place apart just because he thinks he can."

Daniel nodded, the resolve in his voice matching Tom's. "Then we're on the same page. We'll hear what Charles has to say and take it from there. The council might be handling the official investigation, but we both know we can't rely on that alone."

Tom's expression softened again, a faint smile creeping back. "Strange as it feels, I think we make a pretty good team. Maybe we'll surprise ourselves."

Daniel chuckled, the familiar ease of their old friendship warming the moment. "Don't get used to it. I'm still not going fishing with you."

They both laughed, the sound a little easier this time, a reminder of years past when their biggest problems were simpler ones. As they continued down the road, the hum of the truck settled into a comfortable rhythm. They might not agree on everything, but in that moment, they knew they were on the same side, ready to take on whatever lay ahead—together.

***

Tom parked the truck in front of Charles Dixon's office, a modest, unassuming building wedged between two taller ones. He glanced at Daniel, tension still lingering between them from the drive.

"Let's get this over with," Tom muttered, stepping out and striding ahead, his mind set on getting answers. Daniel followed, taking a deep breath as they entered the office, bracing himself for whatever Dixon had to share.

Inside, the receptionist greeted them with a polite smile and led them down a narrow hallway to Dixon's office. The room was small but meticulously organized, with bookshelves crammed with files and a few awards lining the walls. At the desk sat Charles Dixon, a sharp-eyed man with a solid build and graying hair that gave him an air of authority. His gaze softened as he saw Daniel, standing to greet him with a warm smile.

"Daniel," Dixon said, stepping forward to embrace him. "Good to see you. How's Mary?"

Daniel shook his hand and returned the hug, offering a brief smile. "Mary's doing well, Charles. This is my friend Tom Hunter. We're here because we need your help—Carter's Creek is facing a mess with Kevin Pollard's project, and from what I understand, you're familiar with his type of operation, plus we found that you're a frat brother with Councilman Jenkins, who seems entangled with Kevin's project as well."

Dixon's friendly demeanor vanished at the mention of Kevin's name, his expression turning cold. "Kevin Pollard," he repeated, his voice laced with contempt. "Yes, we've crossed paths. Ambitious, arrogant, and about as crooked as they come. I'm still cleaning up the mess he left in my town. I take it you want to know how to stop him?"

Daniel nodded, glancing at Tom before turning back to Dixon. "Exactly. If we don't intervene soon, he's going to drag our town into ruin. We need to know where he's vulnerable."

Dixon's eyes flicked to Tom, sizing him up before he gestured to the chairs in front of his desk. "Take a seat," he said, walking over to one of his bookshelves. "I've dealt with men like Kevin before, but he's in a league of his own. He's smart, but he's made mistakes—mistakes we can use."

Tom leaned forward, his gaze unwavering. "What kind of mistakes?"

Dixon reached up, pulling a folder off a high shelf, his movements slow and deliberate. "Bribes, for one. Shady deals with contractors and suppliers. His tactics are always under the table, but that's not his biggest weakness. Here's the catch—Kevin's been making bad investments, and now he's desperate for cash. This next development? It's make-or-break for him. If he loses this project, he loses everything."

Tom frowned, skepticism written on his face. "And we're supposed to believe that Kevin's big empire depends on a single project? Seems risky, even for him."

Dixon smiled faintly, a glint of satisfaction in his eyes. "Exactly. He took some big swings, and he overextended himself. If his investors pull out, he won't have the funds to keep the project afloat. The whole thing will crumble like a house of cards."

Daniel raised an eyebrow. "So, how do we make that happen?"

Dixon sat back, his face hardening. "Simple: convince the investors that Kevin's running a scam. Show them that he's burned bridges and that his promises are empty. They'll cut him off, and without their cash, Kevin's project collapses. I can give you the names of key investors, but it's on you to get them to listen."

Tom exchanged a glance with Daniel, still slightly skeptical. "Why are you handing over this information so easily, Dixon? What's in it for you?"

Dixon's face grew colder, his voice bitter. "Kevin burned me too, gentlemen. I believed his promises. I thought his plans would benefit my town, but instead, he used it as his personal cash cow. I trusted him, and he turned my support into leverage to squeeze out the locals, my friends. I want him to pay for that, and if you're willing to do what's necessary, I'll gladly help."

Daniel studied Dixon, sensing the man's anger simmering beneath the surface. "We're willing, but let's be clear—our goal is to protect Carter's Creek, not just ruin Kevin. We need your help to make this a reality."

Dixon nodded slowly, handing the folder to Daniel. "Inside, you'll find names, contact information, and a record of every underhanded deal Kevin pulled in my town. It's enough to raise red flags with his investors. But make no mistake—Kevin's ruthless, and he won't hesitate to retaliate. Once you start pulling on this thread, he'll come after you. Are you prepared for that?"

Tom's gaze hardened, his voice resolute. "We're not scared of Kevin. We just want to make sure he doesn't ruin Carter's Creek the way he's hurt other towns."

Dixon gave a tight nod, his expression steely. "I get it, Tom. And I'll tell you this—Jenkins isn't just some casual connection for Kevin. I know Jenkins from way back, and he's got his own stake in keeping Kevin happy. I don't think you'll get him to back down unless his back is against the wall."

Daniel's brow furrowed, absorbing this new revelation. "So Jenkins has a personal interest in all this, not just a professional one. That complicates things. But it also means we know where to apply pressure."

Dixon's expression softened, a hint of respect in his eyes. "Then we're on the same page. Use the information wisely—and watch your backs."

Daniel glanced down at the folder in his hands, feeling the weight of what lay ahead. "Thank you, Charles. This gives us a fighting chance."

Dixon nodded, his tone somber. "Just remember, once you open this door, there's no going back. Kevin's downfall won't be clean. He'll drag anyone he can down with him, and he won't play fair."

Tom smirked, a glint of determination in his eyes. "Good thing neither do we."

The three men stood, a shared understanding passing between them as they shook hands. Dixon's gaze lingered on Daniel, a silent wish for luck passing unspoken. And as Tom and Daniel made their way back to the truck, the significance of the folder in Daniel's hands settled over them both, a reminder that they were about to cross a line—and there was no turning back.

***

Back in the truck, Tom and Daniel settled into a more comfortable silence, the weight of their meeting with Charles Dixon lingering in the air. For the first time in years, they felt like they were on the same page—united for the sake of their town and their families.

After a few miles, Daniel broke the silence, his voice contemplative. "Well, that was definitely a good connection. Now we just need to figure out how to put it all together and keep Kevin from tearing the town apart."

Tom grunted in agreement, nodding as he kept his eyes on the road. "Looks like we're stuck working together longer than either of us planned."

Daniel chuckled, a smile of nostalgia crossing his face. "You know, back in school, I always thought you'd end up running this town—calling the shots, maybe even taking over as mayor. Didn't exactly see you as the tavern type."

Tom let out a laugh, a bit rough but good-natured. "Yeah, well, I guess life threw a few surprises my way too. But you—you? You were such a straight arrow, always doing the right thing, always head buried in books. I'm not even a little surprised you're a pastor."

Daniel smiled, shaking his head. "Guess I was a bit predictable, huh? But you, owning Southern Roots? I would've lost that bet. You were always either chasing girls or making the winning play in a game. The last thing I thought you'd be doing is keeping folks in line at a bar."

Tom chuckled, his grin widening. "Fair enough. But you want to know the real surprise? When the prettiest girl in Carter's Creek, Mary

Parker, decided to marry you." He looked over at Daniel with a teasing gleam in his eye. "Now *that* was something I never saw coming. Mary was practically a legend back then, and here you were, all uptight and serious—and she chose you!"

Daniel's smile softened as he thought of Mary, warmth and pride in his eyes. "Yeah, well, I suppose I got lucky there. Mary always had a way of seeing things most people didn't. She saw me for who I was, and I think... well, I think that's why I've always tried to be the man she deserves."

Tom nodded, his smile less teasing now. "Yeah, she's one in a million, that Mary. You did good, Daniel. Real good."

They lapsed into silence, a shared understanding settling between them. It wasn't the friendship of their youth, but something deeper—an acknowledgment of who they had become and the roles they played in the lives of their families and community.

After a pause, Tom nodded toward the back of the truck. "Got a couple of fishing poles back there. If we've got to talk through a plan, might as well do it the right way. Want to see if the fish are biting?"

Daniel's smile widened, his eyes lighting up at the thought. "Sounds like a good way to go over a plan to take Kevin down. You know... like old times."

The weight of their unspoken history lifted just a little as they pulled off the main road toward the lake they used to fish at together as kids. They found a familiar spot near the water's edge, and within minutes they were casting lines, the quiet splashes breaking the stillness of the lake.

As they settled into the rhythm of fishing, Daniel turned to Tom, his voice reflective. "You know, we had a good thing going back then. But somehow, life happened, and we let it pull us apart."

Tom nodded slowly, reeling his line in a little. "Yeah, I guess we did. Different paths, different choices. But look at us now. Somehow, we found our way back. Maybe not as friends like we were—but as allies, maybe. For the sake of the town, and our kids."

Daniel nodded thoughtfully, gazing out over the lake. "We're both fighting for the same things, even if we don't always agree on how to get there. And, for what it's worth, Tom—I'm glad it's you here. I wouldn't want to face Kevin without you."

Tom looked over, a slight smile touching his face. "Same goes for me. I know you're the right man to get the council moving on this. And... maybe I've misjudged you over the years. You always were the steady one, the one who stuck to what mattered."

They fell into a comfortable silence again, the years between them fading into the background as they watched the water ripple and cast lines into the lake, lost in their thoughts.

After a few minutes, Tom felt the familiar weight of a bite tugging on his line. He grinned, tightening his grip. "Looks like I've got something here."

Daniel glanced over, chuckling. "Haven't lost your touch, huh? Let's see what you've got."

With a satisfied grin, Tom pulled his rod back, reeling in the fish with careful precision. The line danced and the fish gave a good fight, splashing water as it neared the surface. Finally, Tom reeled it in fully, lifting a decent-sized bass out of the water. He held it up, glancing proudly over at Daniel.

Daniel laughed, clapping him on the back. "Not bad. Maybe you're not all talk, after all."

Tom smirked, releasing the fish back into the lake. "Still got it, Pastor."

A moment later, Daniel's line jerked, and he straightened, a glint of excitement in his eyes. "Looks like I've got one, too."

Tom watched, amused, as Daniel carefully reeled in his catch. With a bit of maneuvering, Daniel brought in a decent fish of his own—a little smaller than Tom's, but respectable. He held it up with a grin, his expression equal parts pride and amusement.

"Looks like I haven't lost my touch either," Daniel said, his voice light with satisfaction as he released the fish back into the water.

Tom chuckled, a sense of camaraderie settling between them. "Maybe we've still got a few things in common, after all."

As the sun dipped lower on the horizon, painting the sky in soft hues of orange and pink, the two men continued fishing, exchanging memories and laughter between bites. Each fish reeled in seemed to loosen the grip of the past, mending the unspoken rift between them. They weren't just two old friends who'd grown apart—they were allies, partners, and perhaps, after all these years, friends once again.

***

Luke wiped the sweat from his brow as he stepped back, taking in the progress on the house by the creek. The project was coming along, but his mind wasn't in it today. His thoughts kept drifting to Emma—the way she'd been distant, the concern in her eyes whenever he dodged her questions about his recent absences. The secrecy had felt necessary, but it was creating a wedge between them, and he hated it. Setting his tools down, he decided to take a break and wander down to the creek, hoping the sound of the water might help him clear his mind.

As he neared the creek, familiar voices floated toward him, carrying laughter and a warmth that felt like home. Pushing through the trees, he came upon a surprising sight: his dad, Tom, and Emma's dad, Daniel, sitting side by side on the creek bank with fishing poles in hand, laughing together like old friends. It was a rare sight, and it caught him off guard.

"Well, well, look who's wandered down from his secret project," Tom called out, spotting him first. His dad's face broke into a grin, the kind that Luke hadn't seen in a while.

Daniel waved, motioning for him to join. "Come sit with us, Luke. We've got plenty of room here."

Luke hesitated, unsure about intruding on this unlikely pair. But then Tom held out a fishing pole, giving him an encouraging nod. "Come on, son. Fishing's good for a troubled mind."

Smiling despite himself, Luke took the pole and settled down beside his dad, casting his line into the water. He let the gentle sounds of the creek and the rhythm of casting his line soothe him, grateful for the quiet support.

After a while, Daniel glanced over, breaking the silence. "So, Luke, what exactly are you working on out here by the creek? I don't think Emma's mentioned anything about it to us."

Luke felt his shoulders tense. "Just a project I'm working on. Nothing big."

Daniel raised an eyebrow, his voice light but probing. "Nothing big, huh? Funny thing, when people say that, it usually means it's bigger than they're letting on."

Tom shot Luke a look but said nothing, letting him handle the question. Luke could feel the weight of Daniel's curiosity, and for a moment, he considered sharing more. But he wasn't ready. Not with Daniel, and not with Emma, either.

"I'll tell you more when the time's right," Luke said, trying to keep his tone casual, even though he knew it wasn't the answer Daniel was looking for.

Daniel frowned slightly but nodded, his expression softening. "I respect that, Luke. Just keep in mind that Emma's a good judge of character, and she's been worried. Secrets don't sit well with her. That's how Tom and I ended up here together today—chasing down a way to deal with Kevin and his secrets."

Luke blinked, surprised by the connection. "I knew you two agreed to help with Kevin, but I didn't realize you were already working together."

Daniel nodded, casting his line out again. "Yeah. We're doing our best to stay a step ahead of Kevin's plans. Secrets have a way of unraveling everything if they're left too long."

Tom added, his tone softening, "It's a part of life, son—things get complicated. But the longer you keep a secret, the heavier it gets. And it doesn't just weigh on you; it weighs on the people you care about too."

Luke sighed, staring down at the water. "I know. I don't want to keep Emma in the dark. It's just... complicated right now."

Daniel leaned forward, his voice kind but direct. "Emma's strong, Luke. But she values honesty more than anything. If you really want to protect her, trust her to handle the truth, even if it's difficult."

Their words hit home, each one sinking in deeper than he expected. He hadn't meant to deceive Emma, but maybe he'd misjudged her strength, or maybe he'd been using the complexity of the situation as an excuse to keep things to himself. Either way, it was a sobering realization.

"You're right," Luke admitted after a pause, his voice quiet. "I don't want to mess things up. I just... didn't want to burden her."

Tom nudged him gently. "We all mess up, son. It's what you do afterward that counts."

Daniel smiled, glancing over at Tom. "If Tom and I can figure out how to work together after all these years, I'm pretty sure you and Emma can find your way through this."

Luke chuckled, looking at the two men, side by side, laughing like old friends again. For the first time in days, his path forward didn't seem so clouded. He felt a weight lift, the kind of clarity that only comes from a few honest words and a little push in the right direction.

Tom reeled in his line, inspecting his empty hook with a wry grin. "Fish or no fish, the important thing is to keep moving forward. You've got this, Luke."

Luke stood, feeling lighter than he had in days. "Thanks. Both of you. I think I know what I need to do."

Tom grinned, the warmth in his eyes unmistakable. "Good. Just don't keep her waiting too long."

With one last look at the two dads—fathers of two people who'd somehow ended up on this same winding path—Luke turned and headed back toward the house by the creek. His mind was clearer, his heart more certain, and he knew it was time to finally share his plans with Emma. The future wasn't as uncertain as he'd thought. He had his path, and he knew she'd be waiting, ready to walk it with him.

***

The familiar warmth of the tavern wrapped around them as Emma, Luke, Gabe, and a few close friends settled into their usual booth, the low hum of conversation and clinking glasses adding a comfortable backdrop. Sunlight poured through the windows, casting a golden glow across the room as the sun dipped toward the horizon. Yet, despite the peaceful setting, tension brewed beneath the surface, each of them aware of the trouble stirring in Carter's Creek.

Gabe leaned forward, glancing around to ensure no one else could hear, and lowered his voice. "I overheard something interesting at the bar today. One of the regulars said they saw Linda out by the Old Mill the evening before she disappeared."

Emma's eyes widened. "The Old Mill? What would she be doing out there? That place has been abandoned for years."

Gabe shrugged, his expression puzzled. "No idea. But it was before sunset. After that... no one's seen her."

Luke sat up straighter, a frown tugging at his mouth. "That's strange. The Old Mill's been empty for ages. If she was there, it doesn't make any sense... unless she was meeting someone. Either way, we need to check it out. Maybe there's something there that could help us figure out where she is."

They all exchanged uneasy glances, each of them sensing the gravity of the situation. The thought of Linda, alone at the Old Mill before she vanished, added an eerie layer to the mystery they were already tangled up in.

"Anyway," Luke said, leaning back, "I also ran into my dad and Daniel today."

Emma raised an eyebrow, intrigued. "You did?"

"Yeah," Luke said, a smile breaking through his serious demeanor. "You're not going to believe this—they were fishing together. Actually laughing. It was... weird."

A ripple of laughter moved through the group, breaking the tension as they all pictured Tom and Daniel, fishing poles in hand, side by side by the creek.

Emma grinned, shaking her head in disbelief. "Tom and my dad? Fishing together? That's something I'd pay to see."

Luke chuckled, nodding. "Right? But it wasn't just that. They're actually working together on this Kevin thing, just like they promised. Figured it might be easier if we were all in on it." He glanced toward the back of the tavern, where the staircase led up to Tom's small office. "I asked my dad to come down and fill us in on what he and Daniel found out from Charles Dixon."

As if on cue, Tom appeared at the top of the stairs and made his way over to the group, his expression serious yet softened by a glint of purpose in his eyes. He gave a small nod as he approached, clearly catching the curiosity in the air.

"Dad," Luke said, waving him over, "why don't you give everyone a quick update on what you and Daniel talked about with Dixon?"

Tom nodded and took a seat at the table. "Sure thing." He paused, looking around at the expectant faces, then dove in. "Daniel and I had a good chat with Charles Dixon earlier. Turns out, he knows Kevin pretty well—probably better than anyone would like to. Kevin's pulled some serious stunts in other towns, left people high and dry. But here's the kicker: Kevin's made some bad investments, and now he's desperate for cash. His whole operation depends on the success of this next development. If we can stop his funding, we can shut him down."

Luke leaned in, his voice steady and determined. "That's where we come in. We need to convince his investors that Kevin's running a scam. Charles is helping us make that case."

Tom continued, his tone resolute. "Dixon gave us the names of a few investors—decent men from what he says. If we can show them what Kevin's really up to, we might just get them to pull out before it's too late."

Emma's interest sharpened, and she leaned forward, her voice filled with purpose. "So, we're going after his money? Cutting him off at the source?"

Tom nodded. "Exactly. No cash, no project. But Kevin's a fighter. He's not going to go down without making this as messy as he can. We need to be smart and stay one step ahead."

The table fell quiet as everyone absorbed the weight of what lay ahead. The stakes felt higher now, and each of them knew they had a part to play. Breaking the silence, Gabe leaned forward, his expression resolute.

"So, we focus on his investors—and we need to check out the Old Mill. If Linda was out there, maybe there's something she found... something that might lead us to her."

Luke nodded, his jaw set. "Exactly. It's all connected. Linda's disappearance, Kevin's deal... everything points back to him."

Determination settled over the group as they exchanged looks. They were ready to act, bound together by a shared purpose and a love for their town.

Tom took a final look around the table, his expression uncharacteristically solemn. "You all know what you're getting into here. This isn't just some small-town feud. Kevin's played rough before, and he'll do it again if we get in his way. Just be ready for whatever he throws at us."

Emma met his gaze, her resolve unwavering. "We're ready, Tom. He's taken enough from this town. We're not about to let him take any more."

Luke gave her a nod of agreement, a fierce pride filling him as he looked at the friends gathered around them. This was their town, their fight, and they'd stand together to protect it.

They exchanged a last round of determined glances, silently committing to the plan. The sunset cast a warm, golden light over the room, but the air held a sense of purpose and urgency. Whatever came next, they knew they were ready to face it—together.

Chapter Thirteen
Disappearances & Hidden Agendas

THE NIGHT HAD SETTLED into a heavy dusk, casting an eerie stillness over the Old Mill. Luke, Tommy, and Gabe moved across the overgrown gravel, their flashlights cutting through the murky shadows. The mill, once a thriving hub of the town, now stood as a crumbling monument, it's walls groaning softly in the breeze.

"This place gives me the creeps," Tommy muttered, his flashlight sweeping through the dense, dark corners.

Luke nodded, eyes focused on the looming structure ahead. "Yeah, but if the rumor's true, Linda was last seen here. We have to check it out."

"Linda, here? Alone?" Gabe shook his head, scanning the derelict surroundings with unease. "Who would be following her, and why would she come all the way out here to hide?"

They approached the entrance cautiously, Luke pushing the door open with a loud creak that echoed into the empty expanse of the mill. Inside, the desolate interior was as haunting as they'd expected – broker beams, scattered debris, and years of neglect had left the place in ruins. Dust swirled in the beam of their flashlights as they moved inside, casting ghostly shadows on the cracked walls.

"Linda?" Luke called out, his voice bouncing off the empty, hollowed-out room.

Only silence answered.

They stepped further into the mill, their flashlights sweeping over piles of debris and remnants of long-forgotten machinery. The air grew thicker with each step, a sense of foreboding settling over them as their beams landed on crumbling structures and shattered windows.

Tommy's voice was quieter now. "This doesn't feel right. Why would she stay here, of all places?"

Gabe's flashlight scanned the ground, catching a faint trail of footprints in the dust, leading deeper into the mill. "Look, someone's been through recently."

They followed the tracks, moving carefully, the darkness pressing in around them. The deeper they ventured, the more desolate the place felt, until –

"Luke ... ?" A faint trembling voice broker through the silence.

All three froze, flashlights darting toward the sound. Their beams landed on a figure crouched behind a pile of old crates – Linda. Her face, illuminated by the harsh lights, was pale, her eyes wide with fear.

"There she is!" Tommy whispered urgently, moving quickly beside her. "We've been searching everywhere for you! Are you okay?"

Linda's voice trembled as she hugged herself tightly. "Boy, as I glad it's you guys! I ... I was walking home from the bar when someone started following me. I panicked and pepper-sprayed them."

Gabe leaned in, his voice gentle. "Did you recognize who it was?"

Linda shook her head, eyes darting nervously to the shadows around them. "No ... I didn't see their face, just heard footsteps. After

I sprayed them, I ran. Didn't know where to go, so I just keep running. Eventually, I tripped and sprained my ankle."

She shifted, and Tommy's flashlight revealed her swollen ankle.

"I couldn't keep going, so I hid here in the mill. It was the only place I could think of." Her voice barely a whisper as she added, "I didn't want them to find me. "

Luke frowned, glancing around the abandoned building. "How have you managed out here for days? No food, no water?"

Linda nodded, hugging herself tighter. "There's a rain barrel outside. I've been drinking from that. And, I had a granola bar – it only lasted a day. After that, I just stayed hidden, too scared to leave."

Tommy's expression softened as he put a hand on her shoulder. "You did what you had to do. You're safe now."

Gabe's jaw tightened as he scanned the darkness around them. "Whoever it was, they're still out there. And, if they followed you – they're not going to get away with it."

Luke's gaze turned serious, "We'll get you somewhere safe, Linda. But whoever's behind this – they're not going to get away with it."

Linda nodded shakily, letting out a breath. "Just don't let them find me."

"We won't," Gabe reassured her. "But let's get moving, before anyone else shows up."

They helped Linda to her feet and supporting her weight, their flashlight beams guiding them out of the Old Mill. The night air hit them as they stepped outside, their flashlight beams gilding them out of the Old Mill. The night air hit them as they stepped outside, but the weight of what had happened settled over them like a cloud. Whoever had been following Linda was still out there – and they needed to find out who. Time to call Emma!

***

The group gathered quietly in the parking lot of Old Mill, the shadows from the trees casting long stretches of darkness around them. The risk of being seen in town was too high, and they couldn't afford to draw attention. Linda leaned against the side of the car, her eyes still wide from everything she had just gone through.

Emma approached Linda with a small smile, holding out a bottle of water and a protein bar. "Here you need this," she said gently. "You must be starving."

Linda took them gratefully, tearing open the wrapper. "Thanks," she whispered, taking a long drink from the bottle. The gesture seemed to comfort her, giving her a moment to gather herself.

"We can't risk anyone finding Linda," Tommy said in a hushed tone, glancing around the group. "Kevin's not going to let this go quietly."

Luke nodded, his expression tense. "We need to get her somewhere safe."

Emma thought for a moment, then her eyes lit up. "My parents' parsonage. It's perfect. No one would think to look for her there, and Mom and Dad will keep her safe."

Linda looked unsure but nodded slowly. "Okay. If you think they won't mind."

"They'll be glad to help," Emma said confidently.

With that decided, the group moved quickly. They couldn't linger any longer. Together, they made their way toward the parsonage, sticking to the quieter streets, the silence around them pressing down as they moved through the night.

When they arrived, the porch light at the parsonage was already on. Emma's mom, Mary, stood waiting at the door, her concern clear, while Pastor Thompson stood beside her, arms crossed but his expression soft.

"Emma filled us in," Mary said gently, stepping forward and taking Linda's hand. "You're safe here. Let's get you inside."

Linda blinked, clearly surprised by Mary's kindness. After feeling rejected by the church for so long, she hadn't expected this warm welcome. Still, the warmth and safety of the parsonage were undeniable, and she followed Mary inside.

The familiar smell of home-cooked food filled the space, the parsonage a refuge from the chaos Linda had been running from. Mary led her to the kitchen, already busy preparing something to eat.

"We'll take care of you, sweetheart, " Mary said as she placed a tray in front of Linda. "You've been through enough."

Meanwhile, Pastor Thompson led Luke and Tommy downstairs to the basement. "This space is quiet, out of the way," he explained, showing them the secluded area. "No one comes down here. She'll be well hidden ... and well fed, if Mary has anything to do with it."

Linda followed down, glancing around. The fear in her heart was beginning to ease, the tension loosening its grip. "I didn't think ... I didn't expect this," she admitted softly.

Mary smiled, as she brought down more food. "You're welcome here, Linda. You always have been."

Luke, Tommy, and Emma exchanged relieved glances, knowing they'd bought themselves some time. Linda was in good hands, and now they could figure out their next move to stop Kevin once for all.

***

With Linda settled safely at the parsonage, Emma and Luke made their way back later the next afternoon. The house was quiet, and they slipped down to the basement where Linda was resting on a small cot. Emma carried a small bag with her, which she handed to Linda as soon as they sat down.

"I brought you a change of clothes," Emma said with a soft smile. "Turns out, we're about the same size."

Linda looked surprised and then grateful as she took the bag. "Thank you, Emma. I didn't even think about clothes... but I've felt grimy since I ran from the bar. I had a nice shower, and your mom loaned me a nightgown and washed my clothes, but a change is great. This is really nice of you."

Emma waved it off. "It's nothing. You need to feel a little more like yourself. And, remember, we're friends."

Linda nodded and set the bag aside for a moment before sitting up straighter. "I'm feeling better, but I'm still scared to death!" she admitted, her voice trembling. "Kevin's not going to stop, and I know there's more I need to tell you."

Luke leaned forward. "We need to know everything, Linda. We're close, but we need more to take Kevin down."

Before she could continue, Emma's phone buzzed in her pocket. She glanced at the screen and then looked at Linda and Luke.

"I need to make a call," Emma said, standing up and stepping away. She dialed the sheriff's number, her voice low but calm as she spoke.

"Sheriff, it's Emma. We found Linda hiding out in the Old Mill, someone was pursuing her, we don't know who. I'm hiding her at my parents' parsonage. She's safe for now, but I need you to keep this under your hat. I trust you, but Kevin's getting desperate, and I don't want word getting out until we have a plan."

The sheriff's voice on the other end was firm. "Understood. I'll keep this quiet. Let me know if you need anything, Mayor."

"Thanks, Sheriff," Emma replied, before hanging up and returning to the group. She shot Luke a look that told him everything was handled. "Okay, Linda. Go on."

Linda's eyes darted between them before she nodded, taking a steadying breath. "I told you most of it—about Kevin's investors pressuring him and how he freaked out about me knowing too much. But there's more to it. Jenkins... he's the one who pushed through those permits for Kevin's project."

Emma's brow furrowed, leaning in. "Jenkins? I knew he was involved, but... why would he help Kevin?"

Linda bit her lip, glancing down before she continued, her voice growing softer. "It's personal for him. After his wife passed away, he just... changed. Losing the election to you was one thing, Emma, but her death pushed him to a breaking point. Kevin must have seen that—saw him as someone he could manipulate, maybe someone with a grudge against you. Jenkins might not even realize how deep he's in."

Luke's jaw tightened as he processed Linda's words. "So Kevin isn't just pushing through permits on his own—he's exploiting Jenkins' pain to get what he wants, and Jenkins is letting him, even if it means hurting the town."

Linda nodded, her voice laced with worry. "Yes. But I don't know how you can use that information. He's still on the council, and he has power."

At that moment, Pastor Thompson appeared at the top of the stairs. "Everything alright down here?" he asked as he descended, his eyes focused on Emma.

"We're fine," Emma replied, her voice steady. "But Dad, we need to fill you in on something important."

Pastor Thompson's expression turned serious as he listened to Linda recount Jenkins' deeper role in Kevin's dealings, his bitterness over losing the mayoral election, and the personal grudge he held against Emma. Pastor Thompson nodded, his face tightening as the pieces began to align.

"Charles Dixon mentioned he had suspicions about Jenkins," Pastor Thompson reflected, "but hearing how Jenkins' grief and bitterness made him susceptible to Kevin's influence adds a deeper layer." He sighed, clearly affected. "It's a reminder of how much grief can drive someone to destructive choices. But if Jenkins is this far in with Kevin, he's already dangerous."

Luke nodded. "That's what we're piecing together. Jenkins has been pushing Kevin's permits through, but his real goal might be revenge on Emma—and by extension, the whole town."

Pastor Thompson's voice lowered as he leaned in, his concern evident. "We can't let this go on. He's dangerous, especially if he's working with Kevin in such a personal, calculated way. Emma, you need to be careful."

"I know, Dad," Emma said. "But we have to be smart about this. We don't have enough to take him down yet."

After a moment of thoughtful silence, Pastor Thompson glanced down at the list of Kevin's investors that Emma had handed him earlier. He wasn't usually one for direct confrontation or private investigations, but he knew that Kevin's plans had serious consequences for the community.

"Emma," he said finally, "I may be able to help indirectly." He pulled out his phone and began dialing a number. "I'm reaching out to an old friend from seminary, Reverend Howard Bennett. He mentioned that his town had some trouble with development recently, and he may have a contact connected to Kevin's investors."

Emma watched as her father waited, the phone pressed to his ear. After a moment, a voice answered on the other end.

"Howard, I hope you're well. I'm calling because Carter's Creek is facing a similar problem to what your town went through," Pastor Thompson explained. "I wondered if you might be able to connect me with one of your contacts. There are rumors here that our council is pushing things through that might be harmful in the long run, and I need to make sure we aren't being misled."

There was a pause on the other end before Reverend Bennett replied, "I think I can arrange that, Daniel. One of the men involved in our situation will be in Carter's Creek later this week. He might be open to a quick meeting if he's aware of your concerns. How should I reach you?"

Pastor Thompson leaned back in his chair, relief mingling with gratitude. "Thank you, Howard. I'll let my daughter, Emma, know. She's the one handling this with the town council, but any guidance or contacts would help."

After hanging up, Pastor Thompson turned back to Emma, Luke, and Linda with a small nod of encouragement. "It's in motion. I'll arrange for Emma to meet with the investor once he's in town."

Emma smiled gratefully. "That's great news, Dad."

Pastor Thompson nodded. "We're getting closer, but we need to tread carefully. Kevin's desperate, and that makes him dangerous."

Chapter Fourteen
Suspicious Minds

KEVIN PACED HIS OFFICE, his mind spinning with unease. The longer Linda stayed missing, the more nervous Jenkins would get, and the more jittery the investors would become. Time was running out, and Kevin needed to get control of the situation before everything unraveled.

He stopped abruptly and picked up his phone, calling for a meeting with his crew. Within minutes, they began filing into his office—a small group of men who had worked with Kevin long enough to know that when he was this tense, things were about to get serious.

Kevin didn't waste time. "Linda's still missing, and that's a problem for us. If she talks, she could ruin everything. I need her found."

One of his men, a burly guy named Ray, raised an eyebrow. "She's just a woman, Kev. How much damage can she really do?"

Kevin's eyes flashed. "More than you think. She knows too much, and Jenkins is getting cold feet. He's already asking questions. If we don't get this under control, the investors will start backing out. I need her found, and I need her found now."

The men exchanged glances, the gravity of Kevin's tone sinking in.

"Split up," Kevin ordered. "I want eyes on every corner of this town. Check every spot she might have run to. Friends, family, anywhere she could be hiding. And I don't care how long it takes—find her."

The crew nodded, already moving toward the door when Kevin's voice stopped them.

"And one more thing," he said, his voice dropping lower. "I need someone to follow Jenkins."

The room stilled.

"Jenkins?" Ray asked, confused. "You think he's gonna bolt?"

Kevin's jaw clenched. "I think he's scared. And scared people make stupid decisions. If he's talking to anyone outside this circle, I need to know. Follow him, and report back to me. I don't want any surprises."

One of the men, a quiet and sharp-eyed guy named Vince, stepped forward. "I'll follow him."

Kevin nodded, his tension easing slightly. "Good. Keep it subtle. If Jenkins knows he's being watched, he'll panic. We can't afford that."

Vince gave a curt nod and left the room, while the rest of the crew dispersed to search for Linda. Kevin sat back down behind his desk, rubbing his temples. He needed to find Linda before Jenkins broke under the pressure. If Jenkins started talking, everything they'd built would collapse, and Kevin couldn't let that happen.

As his crew left to carry out his orders, Kevin leaned back in his chair, his eyes narrowing. He would find Linda. And once he did, he'd make sure she never threatened his plans again.

***

The morning sunlight streamed through Emma's office window as she worked through the latest town updates, her mind distracted by all that had been happening. She barely heard the soft knock on her door before it swung open.

There stood Luke, a bouquet of handpicked wildflowers in hand, his usual easy smile on his face.

"Hey," he said, stepping inside and holding out the flowers toward her. "Thought I'd brighten your day a little."

Emma's heart softened at the sight of the flowers, the vivid colors reminding her of the simpler times they used to share. She took the bouquet, breathing in the sweet scent of the blossoms.

"They're beautiful," she said with a small smile. "Thank you, Luke."

But as she set the flowers on her desk, her expression turned more serious. She glanced up at him, her brow furrowing slightly. "But... we need to talk."

Luke's smile faltered as he moved closer, sensing the shift in her tone. "What's on your mind?"

Emma leaned back in her chair, her fingers lightly tracing the petals of the flowers. "You've been disappearing a lot lately. Showing up late, too. That's not like you, Luke."

Luke's brow furrowed, but he didn't respond immediately.

"I'm really starting to get worried," she continued. "You've always been someone I could count on, but right now... it's reminding me of the days after you left the last time. I'm not sure what's going on with you. What are your plans after Founder's Day? Do you even have any?"

Luke took a deep breath, stepping closer and resting a hand on her desk. "Emma, I know I've been a little... off lately. But I promise, I'm not doing it to hurt you. I just have a lot on my mind."

Emma looked up at him, her eyes searching his face. "That's exactly what I mean, Luke. I don't know if I can count on you right now, and your actions—well, they're making me even more concerned about that."

Luke sighed, rubbing the back of his neck. "I didn't mean to make you feel like that. I just needed some time to figure things out."

"And?" she pressed. "Have you figured them out?"

Luke hesitated, his eyes lowering for a moment. "I'm close. I just... need a little more time."

Emma shook her head, the frustration evident in her voice. "Luke, you've always been the guy who knows what he wants, who does what he says he's going to do. But lately, I feel like I'm seeing someone else, someone who's unsure and unreliable. If we're going to make this work, I need to know you're in it, really in it."

Luke's gaze softened as he looked at her. "I care about you, Emma. More than you know. And I want to be here for you, to be someone you can rely on. I just... I have a lot to work through."

Emma nodded slowly, her fingers still idly playing with the flowers. "I want to believe you, Luke. But you need to start showing me that you're serious. After Founder's Day, I need to know what your plans are. I need to know if you're staying or if you're going to disappear again."

Luke swallowed hard, knowing she was right. He had to make a decision—soon.

***

Jenkins sat at the far end of the bar, nursing his third whiskey, his hand trembling slightly as he took a sip. The dim lighting in the tavern couldn't hide the unease etched across his face. He kept glancing around, his eyes darting to the door as if expecting someone—or something—to walk in at any moment.

Behind the bar, Gabe wiped down a glass, watching Jenkins carefully. He'd noticed the man's frequent visits to the tavern lately, and he wasn't one to miss an opportunity. Tonight was no exception.

"Rough day, Jenkins?" Gabe asked casually, setting the glass aside and leaning in a bit closer.

Jenkins grunted in response, taking another sip of his drink.

Gabe, ever the charmer, continued. "You've been looking a little on edge lately. Something going on at the council? Or is it that big project Kevin's got going?"

Jenkins stiffened slightly at the mention of Kevin, his eyes flicking toward Gabe. "Everything's under control. No need to talk about Kevin."

"Of course, of course," Gabe said with a slight grin, noting Jenkins' defensive tone. "But you know how small towns are. People like to talk, and lately, all the talk has been about Linda. You wouldn't happen to know anything, would you?"

Jenkins' grip on his glass tightened, his knuckles white. He looked away, his voice quieter, as if he wasn't sure he should say anything. But after a long pause, he exhaled heavily. "Kevin's losing it, Gabe. I don't know how much longer this whole thing can hold together."

Gabe leaned in, intrigued. "Losing it? How?"

Jenkins glanced around the empty tavern, then leaned in closer, his voice barely a whisper. "He's desperate to find Linda. She knows too much. If she talks... everything we've been doing could blow up. And the investors are starting to get nervous. Kevin's afraid if they start pulling out, he'll lose everything."

Gabe raised an eyebrow. "Investors pulling out? What's Kevin been promising them?"

Jenkins took another sip of whiskey, his nerves showing. "More than he can deliver, if you ask me. The whole deal's been shaky from the start, but now... now it's falling apart. Kevin's banking on this development to save his neck, but if Linda spills what she knows ..."

Jenkins trailed off, his face pale. He'd said too much already, but Gabe wasn't letting up.

"So, what's Linda got on him?" Gabe pressed. "What could she say that would ruin him?"

Jenkins looked at Gabe, his eyes wide with fear. "She knows about the bribes, the deals... everything. And Kevin's been keeping secrets from the investors too. If they find out what's really going on, they'll pull out faster than you can blink."

Before Gabe could push further, the door to the tavern swung open, and in walked Sadie, Tommy, and Hannah. Their laughter filled the room for a moment, but they quickly noticed Jenkins and his uneasy posture. Without hesitation, they made their way over to the bar.

"Well, look who we have here!" Tommy said, clapping Jenkins on the back, though the cheeriness in his voice didn't quite match the tension in the air.

Sadie took a seat next to Jenkins, her eyes narrowing slightly. "You alright, Jenkins? You look like you've seen a ghost."

Hannah pulled up a stool, giving Gabe a quick smile before focusing on Jenkins. "Yeah, what's got you so spooked? You're usually not this quiet."

Jenkins shifted uncomfortably, his eyes darting between them all. "It's... nothing. I just... I just don't like what's happening around here lately."

"Like what?" Sadie asked, leaning in. "The project? Or something else?"

Jenkins swallowed hard, his gaze falling to his half-empty glass. "Linda's still missing. And I... I don't know where she is. It's got me worried, you know?"

Tommy exchanged a quick glance with Sadie before speaking up. "Has anyone heard anything from her at all? I mean, someone has to know something."

Jenkins shook his head, his voice shaky. "No, nothing. And that's what's scaring me. She's been gone too long. If... if something's happened to her — worse if she talks ... " He cut himself off, realizing he'd said too much again.

Gabe's eyes flickered with interest. "Talks? About what?"

Jenkins looked up, his face pale. "I just meant... if she's in trouble and she tries to get back, she could... say things. Things that might make this whole situation worse."

Sadie raised an eyebrow. "Sounds like you're worried about more than just Linda's safety, Jenkins."

Jenkins didn't respond, instead gulping down the rest of his whiskey in one swift motion. He set the glass down with a loud thud and stood up abruptly. "I need to go. I shouldn't have said anything."

Before anyone could stop him, Jenkins stumbled toward the door, his fear palpable as he disappeared into the night.

The group sat in silence for a moment before Hannah broke it. "Well, that was... strange."

Gabe leaned back against the bar, a sly grin on his face. "Strange, indeed. Seems like our friend Jenkins is in over his head."

Sadie nodded thoughtfully. "And if Jenkins is that scared, something big is coming."

***

The basement of the parsonage was warmer than usual, the cozy atmosphere somewhat in contrast to the tension that lingered in the air. Linda sat on the couch, her feet curled underneath her, as the group began to trickle in, each carrying pizza boxes and sodas.

Sadie was the first to smile as she set the boxes on the small table in front of Linda. "We thought you could use a little pizza to brighten your night. Even if we can't fix everything right away, we figured some greasy comfort food might help."

Linda's lips curled into a faint smile. "You guys didn't have to do this."

Tommy shrugged, opening a box. "Of course we did. What are friends for?"

Hannah passed around plates as everyone gathered in a rough circle on the floor and around the couch. Luke sat down next to Emma, his fingers brushing hers as he leaned in close. "We thought it'd be good to catch up. See what everyone's heard, and maybe... figure out a plan."

Linda blinked, setting down her drink. "A plan? For what?"

"To take Kevin down," Emma said firmly, setting her slice of pizza aside. "We know he's desperate, but if we can trap him somehow, use what we know against him..."

"We might be able to get him and Jenkins in one move," Gabe added, leaning back against the wall, arms crossed. "Jenkins has been scared out of his mind, and if we can use that fear, we can push him over the edge."

Sadie raised an eyebrow. "Did Jenkins say anything useful at the tavern? You were working him pretty hard."

Gabe nodded. "Oh, he spilled. He's terrified of Kevin. He knows if Linda talks, the whole operation could come crashing down. He also hinted that Kevin's been keeping things from the investors. If they find out the truth, they'll pull out, and Kevin will lose everything."

Tommy glanced over at Linda. "That sound about right to you?"

Linda nodded slowly. "Kevin promised the investors big returns, but it was all based on lies. And… the bribes. I wasn't supposed to know, but I overheard some things." She paused, her voice softening. "If they knew, they'd be gone in a heartbeat."

Emma leaned forward, her eyes bright with determination. "Then that's what we do. We find a way to get word to the investors, show them the real Kevin."

"But how do we get close to them?" Hannah asked. "They're not exactly hanging around Carter's Creek."

Luke, who had been quiet until now, spoke up. "My dad might be able to help. He and Pastor Thompson have been talking to one of the investors. If we can get them to meet with us, we might be able to convince them to pull out."

Linda glanced around the room, her voice uncertain. "But what if Kevin finds out? He'll come after all of you. I don't want to drag anyone else into this."

Emma reached out, squeezing Linda's hand. "We're already in this. And we're not letting Kevin hurt anyone else."

Gabe tapped his chin thoughtfully. "We could also use Jenkins. If he's that scared, we might be able to push him to turn on Kevin. He's already cracking."

Sadie nodded. "We need to make him think Kevin's going down, and that his only way out is to help us."

Tommy leaned forward, grabbing another slice of pizza. "So, we play on Jenkins' fear, expose Kevin's lies to the investors, and make them both fall at the same time."

Luke grinned slightly. "Simple, right?"

Linda, still looking uncertain, nodded slowly. "Okay. But if we're going to do this... we need to move fast. Kevin won't sit around forever."

Emma smiled warmly at Linda. "We'll be ready."

The group fell into a more relaxed conversation as they ate, discussing how to execute their plan. But beneath the laughter and light-hearted teasing, there was a shared understanding. The stakes were high, and failure wasn't an option.

***

Daniel and Tom sat in the modest office of the church, across from Mr. Reynolds, a sharp-dressed investor who radiated authority. The sunlight filtering through the window gave the room a warm glow, but the conversation was anything but lighthearted.

Mr. Reynolds leaned forward, his expression serious. "So, Pastor Thompson, I understand there's been some tension regarding the development project in Carter's Creek."

Daniel nodded gravely. "Yes, Mr. Reynolds. We've uncovered some troubling information about how Kevin has been handling things. It seems he's more desperate than we realized, which could affect your investment's security."

Tom jumped in. "It's not just the project. Jenkins—one of our council members—has a personal vendetta against Emma for beating him in the mayoral election. He's been pushing permits through for Kevin to settle a personal score, and things are getting out of control now."

Reynolds' face darkened, leaning back in his chair. "A personal vendetta? That complicates things. If Jenkins is motivated by revenge, it could create real instability in the project."

"That's exactly what we're worried about," Daniel agreed. "We want to make sure that your investment remains safe. Kevin's actions have shown signs of instability, and we believe it could all fall apart if it isn't dealt with quickly."

Mr. Reynolds rubbed his chin, clearly weighing his options. "I'm committed to protecting my investment. If Kevin is losing control of the situation, I'll confront him directly. I want to ensure that my interests are safeguarded—or, at the very least, I'll have my money returned."

Tom nodded firmly. "That's why we're here. If we handle this carefully, we can take both Kevin and Jenkins down at the same time. But we need your help."

Daniel leaned forward, his voice steady. "Timing is crucial, Mr. Reynolds. We'll need to gather more evidence, and when the time is right, we'll move forward. I suggest we wait until I give you the signal."

Reynolds sighed and nodded, though his expression remained serious. "I trust your judgment, Pastor. Keep me informed, and when you're ready, I'll do my part."

Standing, Reynolds extended his hand, and both Daniel and Tom shook it. As the investor left the office, the two men exchanged a look of determination.

"We need to move fast," Tom said. "Kevin isn't going to wait around, and neither can we."

Daniel nodded in agreement. "Let's make sure everything is in place. We don't have much time."

***

The evening air was cool as Jenkins left his office, his usual nervous energy heightened by the feeling that something wasn't right. His eyes darted around the quiet street, searching for anything out of place. He couldn't shake the sensation that someone was watching him.

He walked briskly to his car, glancing over his shoulder more than once. When he spotted a dark sedan parked at the far end of the street, he froze. It hadn't been there earlier, and now he could see a man sitting in the driver's seat, staring in his direction.

Jenkins' heart raced. Kevin had warned him to keep quiet, but now it seemed like Kevin wasn't trusting him either. The man in the car was clearly following him, and Jenkins wasn't going to just let it slide.

Acting quickly, he pulled out his phone and dialed the sheriff's office. His voice was tense but controlled when the dispatcher picked up. "This is Councilman Jenkins. I'm being followed. There's a man parked outside my office, and he's been watching me. Can you send someone to check it out?"

The dispatcher assured him they would send a unit right away. Jenkins hung up and glanced nervously back at the car, the knot in his stomach tightening.

Moments later, the familiar sight of a sheriff's patrol car came into view. It pulled up beside the dark sedan, and two deputies stepped out, approaching the car cautiously.

Vince, who had been trying to stay inconspicuous, stiffened when he saw the deputies approaching. His hand instinctively moved to his waistband, where he kept a gun tucked out of sight. He wasn't expecting this.

One of the deputies knocked on his window. "Sir, can you roll down the window?"

Vince hesitated, his mind racing. If he tried to explain himself, it could backfire. But if he didn't cooperate, things could get worse. His tension must have been obvious, because the deputy's hand moved toward his holster.

"Sir, we need you to step out of the vehicle."

Vince's hand twitched, and the deputies reacted immediately. They opened the door, pulling him from the car before he could respond.

"What the hell—" Vince shouted, but the deputies weren't interested in his protests. They quickly handcuffed him and began searching the car.

One of the deputies patted Vince down and pulled out the gun. "You have a permit for this?" he asked.

Vince glared at him but didn't answer.

The deputy shook his head. "That's what I thought. We're going to need to take you in. You're carrying a firearm without a permit."

As they ran Vince's name through the system, they found more than just the illegal weapon. A warrant had been issued for his arrest in another county for a previous charge. Without hesitation, they bundled him into the back of the squad car, taking him into custody.

Jenkins watched the whole scene unfold from a distance, his heart pounding in his chest. He recognized the man now—one of Kevin's. This was bad. Kevin had sent someone to follow him, probably to make sure he wasn't about to crack. And now Kevin's man had been arrested by the sheriff's office, with Jenkins as the one who had made the call.

He was in deeper than he'd realized.

As Vince was driven away, Jenkins stood frozen on the sidewalk, his mind racing. He needed to think fast—Kevin was going to know that Jenkins had been the one who called the sheriff, and there was no telling how Kevin would react.

This mess was spiraling out of control, and Jenkins knew that if he didn't act soon, it wouldn't just be his career on the line—it could be his life.

***

The late afternoon sun cast long shadows over the rural road as Pastor Daniel Thompson drove with Tom Hunter in the passenger seat. They had just left the meeting with the investor, and the conversation with Mr. Reynolds weighed heavily on their minds. The silence between the two men felt reflective, each of them running over the details of the meeting and the delicate situation they found themselves in.

After a few minutes, Tom broke the silence. "Have you noticed Luke acting a little off lately?"

Daniel glanced at him, curious. "What do you mean?"

Tom shifted in his seat, his brow furrowed. "He's been disappearing a lot. Showing up late. He's been heading out toward the creek more than usual, and it's not like him to be so... secretive."

Daniel nodded, concerned. "Emma's noticed it too. She's asked him, but he hasn't given her much of an answer. It's not like Luke to be evasive."

Tom sighed, running a hand over his face. "I've been thinking the same thing. Something's pulling him away, and I'm not sure what it is. I was hoping it had nothing to do with Kevin, but now I'm starting to wonder."

Daniel gave him a serious look. "We can't let him get caught up in any of this mess. Maybe we should take a drive, see what he's been up to out by the creek. Check some of those backroads he's been using."

Tom nodded in agreement. "Let's do it. I've got a feeling we might find something that will explain why he's been so distant."

They drove in silence for a while, following the winding country roads, keeping an eye out for anything unusual. The quiet of the countryside was almost eerie as the sun began to dip lower in the sky. Just when they were about to give up, they spotted something odd—a man working in the yard of a house set back from the road, trimming hedges and planting flowers.

Tom slowed the car. "That house wasn't under renovation last time I was out here. Who's that guy?"

Daniel peered out the window, squinting. "Let's ask."

They pulled up to the house and parked. As they stepped out of the car, the man turned and gave them a friendly wave, clearly happy to have company. He wore a wide-brimmed hat and had the look of someone who worked outdoors for a living—muscles tanned and dirt under his fingernails.

"Afternoon!" the man greeted them, resting his hands on his hips. "What brings you out here?"

Tom nodded toward the house. "We were just driving by and noticed the work you're doing. Looks good. Are you from around here?"

The man shook his head, chuckling. "Nah, I'm from the next town over. This place belongs to a guy named Hunter. You know him?"

Tom and Daniel exchanged a quick glance, surprise flickering across both their faces. "Luke Hunter?" Tom asked cautiously.

The gardener smiled, not catching the shift in tone. "That's the one. Real nice fella. Hired me to do some landscaping work out here. Told me he wanted the place to look good. Looks like he's fixing it up for something, but I didn't ask too many questions. Just happy to have the job."

Daniel stepped closer, feigning casual interest. "Did he say what he was doing out here? This is a pretty out-of-the-way spot for most folks."

The gardener shook his head again. "Didn't say much, just that he wanted to fix the place up. I figure he's got big plans for it. Nice little spot by the creek, though."

Tom felt a knot form in his stomach. Luke hadn't mentioned anything about this place—nothing about renovations, and certainly not about hiring a landscaper. The secrecy didn't sit well with him.

"Thanks for the info," Tom said, trying to keep his voice steady. "You've done good work."

The gardener tipped his hat, clearly proud of himself. "Thank you. If you ever need anything done, you know where to find me."

As the gardener returned to his work, Tom and Daniel stepped back toward the car. Once they were out of earshot, Daniel spoke quietly, his concern mirrored on Tom's face.

"This is what he's been up to," Daniel said, glancing back at the house. "Renovating a place out here and not telling anyone. What's going on with him?"

Tom shook his head, a heavy sigh escaping his lips. "I don't know. But I think it's time we had a serious talk with Luke. He's hiding something, and it's got to do with this house."

They climbed back into the car, both men feeling the weight of their discovery. Whatever Luke was involved in, it was clear he was keeping it secret from the people who cared about him most. And in a town like Carter's Creek, secrets never stayed hidden for long.

***

The small office in the back of the church was cramped but felt familiar to those gathered there. Pastor Thompson sat behind his desk, while Tom leaned against the doorway. Emma, Gabe, Sadie, Tommy, and Hannah all found places to sit, the weight of the past few days hanging heavily in the air. The tension was palpable, but there was also a sense of anticipation—they all knew this meeting was important.

Tom cleared his throat, drawing everyone's attention. "Thanks for coming on such short notice. Pastor Thompson and I wanted to give you an update on our meeting with one of Kevin's investors."

Emma sat up straighter, her eyes flicking between her father and Tom. "You've spoken to one of the investors?"

Pastor Thompson nodded. "Yes. Mr. Reynolds, one of the major investors in Kevin's project, met with us earlier today. He's agreed to help us confront Kevin and push back on his plans."

Tom picked up the explanation. "The good news is that Reynolds isn't happy with the way Kevin has been running things, and he's concerned that his investment is at risk. He's willing to confront Kevin and demand answers. With his involvement, we have leverage."

Gabe, sitting in the corner with his arms crossed, perked up. "That's huge. If the investors start pulling out, Kevin's done."

Pastor Thompson nodded. "Exactly. But we need to play this carefully. Reynolds agreed to wait until we give the signal. We're trying to gather as much information as possible before we make the move."

There was a murmur of agreement around the room before Gabe spoke again, his tone more serious. "Speaking of information, I had a chat with Jenkins the other night at the tavern. The guy's falling apart."

All eyes turned to Gabe.

"What do you mean?" Sadie asked, her voice concerned.

Gabe leaned forward, elbows resting on his knees. "Jenkins is scared, and it's not just about Linda being missing. He's terrified of Kevin. He didn't say much, but you can tell he knows too much and it's eating at him. If we can push him a little more, he might crack."

Emma nodded thoughtfully, but there was something else on her mind. "That reminds me. Jenkins wasn't just being followed by Kevin's man, Vince. He actually called the sheriff's office about it. Vince got arrested for carrying a gun without a permit, and when they ran his name, they found a warrant for his arrest from another county. He's in jail now."

Pastor Thompson raised an eyebrow. "Kevin's man? Arrested?"

Emma nodded. "Yeah. It looks like Kevin sent Vince to keep an eye on Jenkins, but it backfired. Jenkins must have realized something was up and called the cops. Vince got nervous, and when the deputies showed up, it went sideways fast."

Tom exhaled, shaking his head. "Kevin's losing control. First, his investors start getting antsy, now his guys are getting arrested. We need to move quickly."

Sadie leaned forward. "So, what's the plan?"

Tom glanced at Pastor Thompson, and then back at the group. "The plan is simple. We let the investor confront Kevin, and we're there to back him up. But we need to use Jenkins' fear to our advantage. If he thinks Kevin's going down, he might start talking. And if we can get him to spill, the whole thing comes crashing down."

Gabe nodded in agreement. "Jenkins is already unraveling. One more push, and he might flip on Kevin. If we play this right, we can get him to confess."

Emma looked around at the group, her face serious but determined. "Founder's Day is just around the corner. We need to make sure everything is in place before then. This is our chance to take Kevin down, once and for all."

The room fell into a brief silence, the gravity of what they were planning settling in. Everyone understood what was at stake—not just for the town, but for each of them personally. They had come too far to let Kevin's plans destroy everything they'd worked to protect.

Pastor Thompson stood, breaking the silence. "We're close. Stay alert, stay focused, and be ready. We'll set the trap, and when the time comes, Kevin won't know what hit him."

As the meeting wrapped up, the group began to file out of the church office, their conversations quieter now, each person lost in thought about the plan coming together. Luke lingered near the back of the room, exchanging a few final words with Gabe. His focus was already shifting toward the upcoming confrontation, his mind racing with everything that needed to be done.

Tom watched his son from across the room, his expression thoughtful. As Luke started toward the door, Tom moved in beside him, his hands casually in his pockets. "Hey, Luke," he said in a low voice. "You got a minute?"

Luke glanced at his dad, surprised but curious. "Yeah, sure."

Tom gave a nod toward the open door. "Mind if we take a walk? I just want to talk for a minute."

Luke hesitated for a second, sensing there was something more serious on Tom's mind, but he nodded. "Alright, let's go."

They stepped out of the church together, the late evening air cool against their faces as they walked down the gravel path leading away from the building. For a moment, neither of them spoke. Tom took his time, choosing his words carefully.

After a few beats, Tom finally broke the silence. "You've been spending a lot of time out by the creek lately," he said, glancing sideways at Luke. "I couldn't help but notice."

Luke didn't immediately respond, his eyes focused straight ahead as they walked. "Yeah, I guess I have," he said after a moment, his voice measured.

Tom's gaze sharpened, though his tone remained casual. "There's a house out there. Saw it today, along with the work you've been doing. You've been keeping it quiet."

Luke stopped walking, turning to face his dad. "You went out there?"

Tom nodded slowly. "Pastor Thompson and I took a drive, ended up passing through the backroads. We weren't expecting to find anything, but we saw the place. Talked to the gardener."

Luke's jaw clenched slightly, though he wasn't angry—just caught off guard. "I didn't mean to keep it from you."

Tom shrugged, though his eyes never left Luke's face. "I get it. But you've been distant. It's not like you to disappear like this. Emma's worried, and I am too."

Luke looked down at the ground for a second, collecting his thoughts before speaking. "It's just something I've been working on. A project I wanted to handle on my own."

Tom studied his son for a moment before speaking again, his voice quieter. "That place out there... it's more than just a project, isn't it? You've got plans, and I don't think they're just about fixing up a house."

Luke let out a breath, running a hand through his hair. "Yeah, it's more than just a house. I'm trying to figure some things out for myself, Dad."

Tom nodded, understanding in his eyes. "I get that. But don't shut us out. You don't have to figure everything out on your own. Especially now—with everything that's going on."

Luke met his dad's eyes, the tension between them softening. "I'm not trying to push anyone away, especially not Emma. I just needed to do this my way, you know?"

Tom gave him a small smile, clapping him on the shoulder. "I know. But just remember, you've got people here who care about you. You don't have to carry it all by yourself."

Luke nodded, grateful for his dad's understanding. "I won't forget that."

They stood in silence for a moment, the sounds of the night settling around them. Tom gave his son's shoulder one last squeeze before they turned and began walking back toward the church.

As they approached the church, the quiet between them felt less heavy. Luke knew there was still more to sort out, but for the first time in a while, he felt like he wasn't completely alone in figuring it out.

Chapter Fifteen
The Net Tightens

Kevin paced the room, the walls feeling like they were closing in. He needed to think, but his mind was spinning out of control. His phone buzzed again, another message—this time from one of his remaining loyal guys, Ray. A simple question: "What now?"

What now? Kevin didn't know. But he knew he couldn't just sit here. There was too much at stake. If Vince talked, it wouldn't just ruin the project—it would ruin Kevin. The investors would pull out, the town would turn on him, and everything he'd built would come crumbling down.

He rubbed his temples, trying to calm the storm in his head. There was only one option left. He needed to get to Vince—somehow. Silence him, bribe him, threaten him—it didn't matter. Kevin had to make sure Vince didn't open his mouth. But how? Vince was in jail, and Kevin wasn't exactly on friendly terms with the law.

He grabbed his phone and dialed Ray's number. It rang twice before Ray picked up.

"Yeah, boss?"

Kevin didn't waste time with pleasantries. "I need you to handle something."

Ray's voice was steady, loyal. "What do you need?"

Kevin's eyes narrowed as he stared at the wall, his mind working over the details. "Get to Vince. Before he talks."

Ray hesitated for a moment. "He's in jail, Kevin. That's not going to be easy."

"I don't care how you do it," Kevin snapped. "Just do it. We can't afford for him to turn on us."

Ray's silence on the other end made Kevin's blood boil, but eventually, the man spoke. "Alright. I'll figure something out."

Kevin ended the call and threw the phone down on the desk, his anger boiling over. He couldn't afford to wait for Ray to figure something out—he needed results. And fast.

Desperate times. Desperate measures.

He walked over to the desk, pulling out a drawer where he kept an old pistol hidden under a pile of files. It had been years since he'd even thought about using it, but the weight of it in his hand felt steady, calming. He wasn't sure how things would play out from here, but one thing was clear: if Vince talked, there would be no coming back from it.

Kevin tucked the gun into his waistband, his mind made up. If Ray couldn't fix this, he would. One way or another, he wasn't going down without a fight.

***

Jenkins stood at the entrance of Pastor Thompson's office, his hand hovering over the door for a moment before he finally knocked. His heart was racing, and the weight of his decision to come here felt like a boulder pressing on his chest. He had been spiraling, unsure of what to do, and in a desperate moment, he had found himself seeking the one person in town he thought might help without judgment—Pastor Thompson.

The door opened, and Pastor Thompson stood there, a warm smile on his face. "Jenkins, good to see you. Come in."

Jenkins stepped inside, his hands fidgeting at his sides. The office was quiet, peaceful, and filled with books and framed photos that reflected the pastor's long service in the community. Pastor Thompson gestured to a chair, and Jenkins sat down, feeling the tension in his shoulders ease just slightly.

"I didn't know who else to turn to," Jenkins started, his voice shaky. "I... I just need some wise counsel, Pastor. I'm in over my head."

Pastor Thompson sat across from him, his expression patient and kind. "I'm glad you came. Sometimes, when we're facing something difficult, the first step is just admitting we need help. What's on your mind, Jenkins?"

Jenkins exhaled heavily, his fingers twisting together. "I'm scared. Everything with Kevin, with the project—it's falling apart. And I'm caught in the middle. I never wanted it to get this far, but now... now I don't see a way out."

The pastor nodded thoughtfully, allowing Jenkins to continue. He knew from experience that sometimes people just needed space to talk things through before they could make sense of their situation.

"I've done things I'm not proud of," Jenkins went on. "I've pushed through permits, cut corners, all because Kevin was pressuring me. And now, with Linda missing and Vince getting arrested, I'm worried everything's going to come crashing down. If people find out... if they know what I've done, my name, my reputation—it's all over."

Pastor Thompson leaned forward slightly, his voice gentle but firm. "It sounds like you've been carrying a heavy burden for a long time,

Jenkins. You've made some choices that led you here, but that doesn't mean it's too late to do the right thing."

Jenkins looked down at the floor, his throat tight. "I don't know what the right thing is anymore."

The pastor remained silent for a moment, then asked, "Do you believe that telling the truth could help? That coming forward and being honest about what's happened might allow something good to come out of this bad situation?"

Jenkins swallowed hard, his mind racing. "You mean... testify? Against Kevin?"

Pastor Thompson nodded slowly. "If you were willing to testify, to help expose what Kevin's been doing, you could play a role in turning this around. It won't be easy, and I won't pretend that it won't come with consequences. But it might give you a chance to start fresh, to repair some of the damage, instead of letting things spiral out of control."

Jenkins rubbed his hands over his face, the weight of the decision pressing on him. "If I testify... if I turn against Kevin... it could ruin me. He won't just let me walk away from this."

Pastor Thompson's voice remained calm, offering reassurance. "I won't tell you that this won't be difficult. But I believe there's a chance for redemption here, Jenkins. You have an opportunity to do what's right, even if it's hard. And in the end, that's what people will remember—the courage to stand up and speak the truth."

Jenkins sat back in his chair, staring at the ceiling, his mind a blur of fear and doubt. Could he really turn on Kevin? Could he testify and face the backlash? But deep down, he knew that staying silent would only make things worse.

"I... I don't know if I can do it," Jenkins admitted. "I'm scared, Pastor. I don't know if I have the strength to stand up to him."

Pastor Thompson smiled kindly. "It's alright to be scared, Jenkins. Courage isn't the absence of fear—it's doing what's right even when you're afraid. You don't have to decide right this second. Take some time to think about it. But know that you don't have to face this alone."

Jenkins took a deep breath, nodding slowly. "I'll... I'll think about it."

Pastor Thompson leaned back in his chair, giving Jenkins space. "In the meantime, I'd like to arrange a meeting for you with the city attorney. If you're willing to share what you know, we can explore what options you have. We can do this quietly, for now, until you're ready to take the next step."

Jenkins hesitated, but the pastor's calm presence gave him a sense of hope he hadn't felt in a long time. "Alright. Set up the meeting. But... let's keep it quiet. I don't want Kevin to know."

Pastor Thompson gave him a reassuring nod. "Of course. We'll take it one step at a time."

As Jenkins left the office, the weight of his situation still hung over him, but there was a sliver of relief, knowing that maybe—just maybe—he could find a way out of this mess after all.

***

The soft sound of laughter echoed through the cozy living room of Pastor Thompson's house as Emma, Hannah, Sadie, Mary, and Linda sat around, surrounded by snacks, magazines, and cups of tea. The girls had decided to have a "day in," something to lift Linda's spirits after the whirlwind of emotions and fear that had been swirling around her lately. For the first time in what felt like forever, Linda felt a sense of peace.

Hannah was in the middle of telling a funny story from her childhood, and the room erupted in laughter as she mimicked her younger self. Linda couldn't help but laugh along, her smile bright, but there was something in her eyes—something wistful, almost sad. Emma noticed it first and caught her eye, offering a gentle smile.

"You okay, Linda?" Emma asked softly, her voice cutting through the laughter with a note of concern.

The room quieted as the others picked up on the shift in Linda's demeanor. Linda took a deep breath, setting her tea down on the table in front of her. "I'm okay. I just... I've been thinking a lot lately, about everything. About my life."

The girls exchanged glances, waiting for her to continue.

"I have so many regrets," Linda admitted, her voice softer now. "I've spent so much time chasing after the wrong things. Money, attention... I've made a lot of mistakes. And now, with all this going on, I'm starting to realize how far off track I've gotten."

Sadie reached out, placing a comforting hand on Linda's knee. "We've all made mistakes, Linda. But you're here now, and that counts for something."

Linda smiled, but it didn't quite reach her eyes. "I know. I just wish I had done things differently. I don't want to keep living the way I have. I want to change. I want to do something good with my life, even if it costs me everything."

Emma leaned in, her voice steady and encouraging. "You're already taking steps, Linda. You've been brave, standing up to Kevin. And if you're willing to testify against him, you'll be making a real difference."

Linda's gaze flicked up to Emma, her expression serious. "I've thought about it, and I've decided—I'm going to testify. I'll do whatever it takes, even if it costs me everything."

The room fell silent for a moment, the weight of Linda's decision sinking in. But instead of somberness, there was a quiet sense of admiration and respect for Linda's courage.

"I'm so proud of you," Mary said softly, her eyes shining with warmth. "It takes a lot of strength to stand up and do what's right, especially when it's hard."

Linda nodded, though her emotions were swirling. "Thank you. I'm just... I'm scared. I've been so focused on surviving, on getting by, that I haven't thought much about what I actually want to do with my life. When all this is over, I want something different. Something that feels... right."

Hannah tilted her head, curiosity in her voice. "What do you like to do, Linda? What makes you feel good?"

Linda paused, thinking it over. "I like organizing things. I'm good with paperwork, office work, keeping things tidy. And I like talking to people—being friendly, helping where I can. But I never really had a plan for my life, you know?"

Sadie smiled brightly. "That's great, Linda! Those are really good skills."

Mary's face lit up as an idea came to her. "You know, when all of this is said and done, and things settle down, maybe there's something you could do with those skills. I'm always telling Daniel we could use some help at the church. You'd make a wonderful receptionist—you've got the warmth, the organization, and the way with people. I think it could be a perfect fit."

Linda's eyes widened, clearly taken aback by the suggestion. "Me? A receptionist at the church?"

Mary smiled kindly. "Why not? You'd be helping people every day, welcoming them, keeping things running smoothly. I think it would be a wonderful way to start fresh."

The room seemed to brighten as the idea hung in the air, and for the first time in a long while, Linda felt a glimmer of hope. "I... I'd love that. It sounds like exactly the kind of change I need."

Emma grinned, squeezing Linda's hand. "Then it's settled. When all of this is over, we'll help you get there."

The conversation shifted back to lighter topics, and the laughter returned, but the undercurrent of hope remained. Linda had made her decision, and with the support of her friends around her, she knew that no matter what happened next, she wouldn't face it alone.

***

Luke stood in front of the old barn on the outskirts of town, his hands shoved deep in his pockets, eyes scanning the horizon. The project had been weighing heavily on him for weeks now, and as Founder's Day loomed closer, he knew he couldn't keep it a secret any longer.

He glanced over his shoulder as Tommy and Gabe pulled up in Tommy's truck. The two of them hopped out, walking toward Luke with curious expressions.

"Alright, man," Tommy said, clapping Luke on the shoulder. "You called us out here—what's going on?"

Luke took a deep breath, his nerves rattling a little. "There's something I've been working on. A project. I've been keeping it quiet, but I think you guys already have it mostly figured out."

Gabe raised an eyebrow, a small smirk on his face. "The house by the creek, right? The one you've been sneaking off to every other day?"

Luke chuckled, shaking his head. "Yeah, that's the one."

Tommy crossed his arms, giving Luke a knowing look. "We had a feeling something was up. You've been acting pretty secretive, and Emma's been worried. So, what's the big project?"

Luke took another deep breath before speaking. "I've been working on fixing up the house. It's been a wreck for years, but I wanted to bring it back to life. It's kind of a personal thing... something I needed to do for myself. But I can't finish it on my own, not with everything else going on."

Tommy and Gabe exchanged a quick glance before Gabe spoke up. "Well, why didn't you just ask us for help, man? We've been waiting for you to say something. You know we've got your back."

Luke rubbed the back of his neck, a little embarrassed. "I didn't want to burden anyone. But now I'm running out of time. The deadline is Founder's Day."

Tommy gave him a lopsided grin. "You know we're not going to let you tackle this alone. All you had to do was ask."

Gabe nodded in agreement. "Founder's Day is coming fast, but if we carve out some time, we can get it done. We just need a plan."

Luke felt a wave of relief wash over him. He had been carrying the weight of this project for so long, and now that his friends knew, it didn't feel quite so heavy. "Thanks, guys. I didn't realize how much I needed the help."

Tommy slapped him on the back. "That's what friends are for. Now, let's make a plan and get this thing finished before the big day."

The three of them stood there, hashing out the details—who would take care of what, when they could meet up, and how they'd make sure everything was ready in time for Founder's Day. The sense of camaraderie grew with each word, and Luke felt lighter with each passing minute.

By the time the sun dipped below the horizon, casting the landscape in hues of orange and pink, they had their plan in place. The house would be ready, and Luke would no longer be carrying the burden alone.

Chapter Sixteen
Desperate Moves

KEVIN SAT IN HIS office, the blinds drawn tight, casting the room in shadows. The weight of the last few days had been suffocating, and Vince's arrest was just the start of his problems. Kevin had heard that Vince had been extradited to another city because of an outstanding arrest warrant. Now, Vince was out of his reach, and that terrified Kevin more than anything. If Vince cracked, everything would fall apart.

The phone on his desk buzzed, pulling Kevin from his spiraling thoughts. He grabbed it immediately. It was Ray—his closest guy, though even that didn't feel reassuring anymore.

"What's going on, Ray? Any news on Vince?" Kevin's voice was sharp, the tension palpable.

Ray hesitated on the other end, clearly uncomfortable. "Yeah, we confirmed it. Vince was extradited to another city. He hasn't said anything yet, but... well, it's not looking good."

Kevin slammed his fist on the desk, the frustration building. "And Jenkins? What's going on with him?"

Ray's voice dropped to a whisper, his hesitation evident. "That's... that's where things get tricky, boss. Jenkins is acting weird. Real weird. He's meeting with people, but we're scared to follow him too closely."

Kevin narrowed his eyes. "Why?"

Ray sighed, the sound of someone who knew he was in a no-win situation. "Because Jenkins is the one who got Vince arrested. He's the reason Vince was picked up in the first place. If we get caught following him, it could blow up in our faces again. The crew's on edge—no one wants to end up like Vince."

Kevin's pulse quickened. Jenkins had always been a wildcard, but this? If Jenkins really was working against him, everything Kevin had built would crumble. He stood up, pacing the small office, trying to find a solution. He couldn't afford to lose control now—not when it felt like everything was slipping away.

"I don't care what it takes," Kevin growled, his voice low and dangerous. "We need to know what Jenkins is up to. Get someone on him—someone who won't get caught."

Ray remained silent for a moment, clearly unsure. "Boss... I don't know if that's a good idea. Jenkins is jumpy. If he catches wind of us tailing him again, we might lose him for good."

Kevin stopped pacing, glaring at the phone as if Ray could feel the weight of his stare. "I don't care. Jenkins is too dangerous right now. If he's talking to someone, I need to know who. And I need to know now."

Ray let out a resigned sigh. "Alright. We'll keep an eye on him. But I'm telling you, the crew's nervous. Jenkins is a ticking time bomb."

Kevin hung up the phone, his frustration boiling over. He knew Ray was right—the crew was spooked, and for good reason. Vince had been arrested because Jenkins called the sheriff on him. That had thrown everything into chaos, and now Vince was out of reach in another city, leaving Kevin with even more uncertainty.

He couldn't trust anyone anymore. Not fully.

Kevin walked to the window, parting the blinds just enough to peer out at the quiet street below. It was a far cry from the chaos inside his head. His world was unraveling, and Jenkins was the key to it all.

He picked up his phone again, dialing a number he hadn't used in a long time. It was a last resort, but desperate times called for desperate measures. If Jenkins was talking to someone, Kevin was going to find out. And if he had to get his hands dirty to make that happen, so be it.

As the phone rang, Kevin's mind raced. He couldn't let paranoia get the best of him—not now. But he also couldn't let Jenkins slip away. The stakes were too high.

Someone picked up on the other end of the line. "Yeah?"

Kevin's voice was cold and controlled. "I've got a job for you. It's delicate, but it needs to be done right. Jenkins. Find out who he's talking to—and don't let him see you."

The voice on the other end responded with a gruff, "Understood."

Kevin hung up, sinking back into his chair. His options were dwindling, and he knew it. But he wasn't ready to give up yet. Not by a long shot.

***

Luke stood in front of the house, hands on his hips, surveying the work that still needed to be done. Tommy and Gabe were right behind him, both of them equally focused on the task at hand. The house renovation project was shaping up, but with Founder's Day just around the corner, the pressure was on.

"We've got a lot left to do," Luke said, breaking the silence. "And not much time to get it done."

Tommy wiped his brow and nodded. "We can't slow down. If we're gonna finish this, we'll need to double our efforts."

Gabe cracked a smile, ever the optimist. "Hey, we've pulled off crazier things, right? Let's just set up a plan and get to work."

They huddled together, going over the final details—who would handle what, when they'd be able to meet, and how they could divide their time to get the job done. The house was important, though Luke hadn't explained just how much. All they knew was that the deadline was non-negotiable, and Luke was determined to finish before Founder's Day.

Just as they were wrapping up their conversation, the sound of footsteps on the gravel road caught their attention. Luke looked up to see his dad, Tom, walking toward them, Pastor Thompson not far behind.

"Well, well," Tom said, his voice carrying a hint of amusement. "I figured you three were up to something."

Pastor Thompson offered a warm smile, though there was curiosity in his eyes. "You boys have been spending a lot of time out here. We thought we'd come see what you're working on."

Luke exchanged a quick glance with Tommy and Gabe, unsure how much to say. The project was personal, but he couldn't deny that the extra hands would help. Still, he wasn't ready to spill everything just yet.

"We're working on getting this house fixed up," Luke said, keeping his tone casual. "Got a tight deadline, though."

Tom raised an eyebrow. "Tight deadline, huh? And I'm guessing that deadline is Founder's Day?"

Luke nodded. "Yeah, we're trying to get it finished by then."

Pastor Thompson stepped closer, his gaze thoughtful. "We suspected the three of you were working together on something like this. But what's the rush? What's the bigger picture here?"

Luke hesitated, not wanting to reveal too much. "Let's just say it's part of a bigger plan I've been working on. Something important. I'll explain more when the time's right."

Tom crossed his arms, looking his son up and down. "Fair enough. But if you're in a hurry, why don't you let us pitch in? We've got experience with this kind of thing, and you could use the help."

Luke glanced at Tommy and Gabe, who both shrugged, clearly on board with the idea. He turned back to his dad and Pastor Thompson. "Alright. We could use the help. But we need to keep moving fast. There's no time to waste."

The two older men smiled, rolling up their sleeves and getting ready to work. As they joined in, the energy around the house shifted. With everyone working together, it felt like the project was finally moving at the pace it needed to. But even as they worked, Luke couldn't shake the feeling that this project was about more than just the house—it was about the future he was trying to build, a future he wasn't ready to fully share just yet.

***

Linda sat nervously at the kitchen table, her hands twisting together as Emma, Mary, and the other girls gathered around her. It was a quiet, supportive space—exactly what she needed right now. They'd been talking about the upcoming testimony for a while, but as the court date loomed closer, Linda's anxiety grew.

"I don't know if I can do this," Linda admitted, her voice trembling slightly. "What if they ask me something I'm not ready for? What if I mess it all up?"

Emma leaned forward, her tone gentle but firm. "Linda, you're stronger than you think. You've come this far, and we're all here to help you through it."

Hannah nodded, offering a soft smile. "You're not alone. We've got your back every step of the way."

Mary, sitting beside Linda, reached out and placed a hand on her arm. "The key is being prepared, dear. The truth is on your side, but the courtroom can be intimidating. That's why we're going to make sure you're ready for anything they throw at you."

Linda took a deep breath, her hands still fidgeting. "I'm scared. Not just of Kevin, but of everything—what this will do to my life after all of this is over."

Mary's expression softened, and she spoke with a calm, spiritual wisdom that Linda had come to rely on. "It's alright to be scared. Doing the right thing doesn't mean it's easy. But the truth is what sets us free, even when it feels like the hardest thing to do."

Linda met Mary's eyes, feeling both comforted and a little more grounded by her words.

"Let's start with the basics," Mary continued, pulling out some notes they had made earlier. "They'll ask you about your relationship with Kevin, and about the deals you know he's been making. We'll go over what you need to say, how to keep calm, and how to respond when the questions get tough."

They began rehearsing, with Emma playing the role of a tough attorney, asking direct and uncomfortable questions. At first, Linda stumbled over her words, her nerves getting the better of her. But with each round of practice, she found her voice growing stronger, more confident. Mary would gently guide her back when she faltered, offering spiritual encouragement to keep Linda focused on the bigger picture.

"You've lived through a lot," Emma said after a particularly tough round of questioning. "But you're still here. You're still standing. You've got the strength to get through this, I know you do."

Linda nodded, though a tear slipped down her cheek. "I want to do the right thing. I really do. But I'm terrified."

Mary squeezed her hand gently. "Courage isn't about not being afraid, Linda. It's about doing the right thing even when you are afraid. You're stepping into the light, and that takes real bravery."

The girls gathered closer, their support like a steady anchor for Linda as she prepared for the battle ahead.

As they continued to rehearse, Linda's fears began to shift, transforming into a quiet determination. She wasn't alone in this fight, and with the support of these women—her friends—she was ready to face whatever came her way.

***

The small conference room in the back of the law office was quiet, the air thick with tension. Pastor Thompson sat beside Jenkins, offering a calm and reassuring presence. Across the table, the city attorney, Mr. Wheeler, a sharp-looking man in his late 40s, leafed through a small stack of papers, his glasses perched low on his nose. Jenkins sat stiffly, his hands clasped tightly in front of him, nerves visible in the tightness of his jaw.

Pastor Thompson glanced at Jenkins, giving him an encouraging nod. "It's alright, Jenkins. You're doing the right thing."

Jenkins swallowed hard, but he nodded. "I know. It's just... I'm not sure how this is all going to play out. Kevin doesn't just let people walk away. And if I testify—" He stopped, the weight of the situation hanging in the air.

Mr. Wheeler leaned forward, folding his hands on the table. "I understand this is a difficult position you're in, Mr. Jenkins, but we have ways to protect you. The more information you provide, the better your chances are for securing a deal that minimizes your exposure."

Jenkins shifted uncomfortably in his chair. "I didn't want things to get this far. But I'm in too deep now. I know things—things that could bring Kevin down. But I also know what he's capable of, and that's what scares me."

Mr. Wheeler studied Jenkins for a moment before responding. "You've already taken the first step by coming here. If you're willing to testify, to help expose what Kevin's been doing, you could play a pivotal role in turning this around. It won't be easy, and I won't pretend that it won't come with consequences. But it might give you a chance to start fresh, to repair some of the damage, instead of letting things spiral out of control."

Jenkins rubbed his hands over his face, the weight of the decision pressing on him. "If I testify... if I turn against Kevin... it could ruin me. He won't just let me walk away from this."

Pastor Thompson's voice remained calm, offering reassurance. "You're not alone in this. The truth is coming out, and it's better if you're the one helping to reveal it, rather than being caught in the fallout."

Mr. Wheeler interjected, his tone more formal. "Mr. Jenkins, for you to receive immunity, we need a full confession of all your actions and motives related to Kevin and the project. This includes any illicit activities you were involved in and the reasons behind your decisions. In exchange, your immunity is contingent upon the information you provide leading to Kevin's arrest and conviction."

Jenkins looked taken aback, his fear deepening. "So, I have to tell everything?"

Mr. Wheeler nodded. "Yes. You need to lay out every detail, no matter how small. The more comprehensive your testimony, the stronger the case we can build against Kevin."

Jenkins glanced at Pastor Thompson, who gave him a reassuring smile. "It's a big step, Jenkins. But it's the right one."

Jenkins took a deep breath, nodding slowly. "Alright. I'll testify. I'll give you everything I know. I just... I need to make sure my family is safe."

The city attorney nodded, his expression softening slightly. "We'll take care of that. The more cooperative you are, the stronger our case becomes, and the better we can protect you legally."

Jenkins glanced at Pastor Thompson again, who smiled gently. "You're doing the right thing, Jenkins. And we'll all be here to support you through this."

Jenkins finally seemed to relax a little, though the tension still lingered in his eyes. "Okay. Let's do this."

Mr. Wheeler leaned forward, outlining the next steps. "We'll arrange for you to meet with our witness protection coordinator. They'll discuss the specifics of your protection and any other needs you might have. Additionally, we'll need detailed information about your involvement and Kevin's operations. The more precise you are, the better we can ensure your safety and build a solid case against him."

Jenkins nodded, the gravity of the situation settling in. "I'll gather everything I have. Emails, transaction records, any communications I had with Kevin and his associates."

Pastor Thompson placed a hand on Jenkins' arm, his voice soft but steady. "Take your time, Jenkins. We're here to help you every step of the way."

Jenkins let out a shaky breath, feeling a small sense of relief amidst the chaos. "Thank you, Pastor. And thank you, Mr. Wheeler. I hope this can finally put an end to all of this."

Mr. Wheeler stood, extending his hand. "We appreciate your cooperation, Mr. Jenkins. Together, we can bring Kevin to justice and help you rebuild your life."

As Jenkins shook his hand, he felt the weight of his decision but also a flicker of hope. The path ahead was daunting, but for the first time in a long while, he felt like he had a chance to make things right.

Chapter Seventeen
Founder's Day Preparations

THE TOWN SQUARE BUZZED with activity as vendors set up booths and decorations went up in every corner. Founder's Day was just two days away, and the final details were falling into place. Amid the hustle, Emma stood with Sadie and Hannah by the gazebo, checking off items on a long to-do list.

"Okay, that's the last of the vendor permits," Emma said, tapping her pen against the clipboard. "We just need to finalize the schedule, and I think we're good for now."

Hannah, ever the optimist, gave a wide grin. "It's all coming together! This year's Founder's Day is going to be amazing. I can feel it."

Sadie laughed as she stacked flyers on a nearby table. "I just hope the weather holds up. The only thing we can't control."

Emma nodded, distracted by the whirlwind around her, but her thoughts were elsewhere. She glanced over at the creek, remembering the last time she and Luke stood there together. The memory tugged at her heart, and before she could stop herself, she sighed.

Hannah, ever observant, picked up on the shift in Emma's mood. "What's going on with you, Emma? You've been lost in thought for the past hour."

Emma hesitated, her fingers playing with the edge of the clipboard. "It's just... it's Luke. I don't know what to think anymore."

Sadie exchanged a knowing look with Hannah and stepped closer. "Go on. We're listening."

Emma leaned against the gazebo rail, staring out at the bustling square. "It's so hard to explain. I'm trying to focus on getting everything ready for tomorrow, but I can't stop thinking about him. I've been remembering how things were between us when we were younger. How easy it felt back then—how sure I was about him."

Hannah smiled gently. "You two were something special, back in the day. It's no surprise those memories are coming back."

Emma nodded, but her expression clouded. "But then... he left. And it wasn't easy after that. I told myself I was over it, over him. But now that he's back, I can't shake this feeling. It's like... everything's getting mixed up with the fact that he left me once. Why can't it just be easier this time?"

Hannah crossed her arms, leaning against the rail beside her. "Sometimes, love doesn't make sense. It's messy. But that doesn't mean it's not real."

Emma bit her lip, her frustration evident. "I keep telling myself that, but every time I start to let my guard down, I remember—he left before. What if he leaves again? What if this is all temporary?"

The vulnerability in her voice was palpable, and Sadie placed a hand on her arm. "What's he up to, anyway? Is he really thinking about staying this time?"

Emma sighed. "I don't know. He's been working on something—he's always busy, always sneaking off to work on whatever this big project of his is. He won't tell me what it is, and it's driving me crazy."

Hannah chuckled. "Sounds like Luke. Always the wanderer."

Emma shook her head. "It's more than that. If he leaves again... it's going to hurt. A lot. Because I think... no, I know—I'm in love with him. But..."

She paused, uncertainty clouding her features.

Sadie raised an eyebrow. "But what?"

Emma's voice softened. "Maybe it's not love. Maybe I just needed him right now. He's been there for me through all of this with Kevin—he's been my rock. Maybe I'm just clinging to that support. It's hard to tell if my feelings are real or if I just needed someone strong beside me."

Hannah leaned in. "It's possible. But don't underestimate how much history you two have. Support is important, but it doesn't mean your feelings aren't real."

Emma nodded slowly, but the doubt remained in her eyes. "I just don't know. It's all so mixed up. And if he leaves again... I don't think I can go through that twice."

Sadie gave her a reassuring smile. "Whatever happens, we're here for you. You don't have to figure it all out right now."

Emma smiled softly, grateful for her friends, but the uncertainty in her heart lingered. Founder's Day was supposed to be a celebration, but for her, it felt like everything was hanging in the balance—her feelings for Luke, the future, and whether she could trust herself to know the difference between love and support.

***

Kevin paced back and forth in his office, his thoughts racing. Founder's Day was just two days away, and everything felt like it was slipping out of control. Vince was still in custody, Jenkins was a loose cannon, and Linda's whereabouts were a mystery. His plans were unraveling, and he needed answers—fast.

He snatched up his phone and dialed a number. It rang twice before a familiar voice answered.

"What've you got for me?" Kevin demanded, his frustration clear.

There was a pause on the other end. "Not much yet. Jenkins has been keeping his distance. He knows someone's watching him. It's hard to get close."

Kevin's jaw clenched. "I don't care how careful he's being. You need to find out what he's up to. If he flips, we're both done."

The informant's voice was calm, too calm. "Why are you so worried about Jenkins? You think he's going to turn on you?"

Kevin stopped pacing, the question making him bristle. He didn't trust Jenkins any further than he could throw him, but admitting that out loud felt like weakness. "Jenkins is the one who got Vince arrested. You don't think that's enough to be worried about?"

Another pause, and the informant pressed further. "So, if Jenkins talks, what's the plan? How do you keep him quiet?"

Kevin's mind raced as he thought about how deep Jenkins was in with him. "He won't talk. He's in too deep. But if he does, I'll make sure he regrets it."

The informant's tone was smooth, digging deeper. "You've been paying him to keep this quiet, haven't you? Is that how you plan to handle it again?"

Kevin sneered. "I'm not paying Jenkins any more than he deserves. He pushed those permits through, didn't he? That's all he's good for."

FOUNDER'S DAY PREPARATIONS   183

The informant's voice lowered. "Speaking of payments... when am I getting mine?"

Kevin rubbed his temples, the tension rising again. "You'll get paid when this is over. Don't worry about that. I've got a way to move the money—clean as a whistle. You'll get your cut."

The informant paused, waiting for more. "And how's that going to work?"

Kevin's lips twisted into a smirk. "Let's just say I've got a few business ventures that make it easy to shuffle things around. No one's gonna notice. You'll get paid through the usual channels—clean, like always."

Satisfied with his answer, the Informant let the conversation linger for a moment. "Alright. Just making sure I don't get left out in the cold. You know how these things go."

Kevin grunted. "You won't. Just get Jenkins under control and make sure Vince stays quiet. I don't care how you do it—just get it done."

With that, Kevin hung up the phone, tossing it onto his desk. He stared out the window, his mind racing. Every move felt like it was teetering on the edge of collapse, and with Founder's Day so close, time was running out to save his project—and himself.

He had no idea that the conversation he'd just had wasn't as private as he thought. As far as Kevin was concerned, he was still pulling the strings. But for how long?

***

Jenkins sat in the back pew of the small church, staring up at the stained glass window, lost in thought. The light filtering through the glass painted colors across the wooden floors, but Jenkins couldn't see the beauty in it. All he felt was the weight pressing down on him—guilt, shame, and fear. His involvement with Kevin had led him down a dark path, and now that path was closing in on him.

Pastor Thompson entered quietly, noticing Jenkins' slumped posture. He walked over and sat beside him without a word, waiting for Jenkins to speak.

After a long silence, Jenkins finally exhaled. "I don't know if I can do this, Pastor. I thought... I thought maybe if I just stayed quiet, everything would blow over. But it's not. It's getting worse."

Pastor Thompson placed a comforting hand on his shoulder. "Doing the right thing is never easy, Jenkins. It takes courage. But you know deep down what needs to be done."

Jenkins swallowed hard, his voice barely above a whisper. "I don't even know if God could forgive me for what I've done. My envy, my hate—it's what got me here. I wanted what I didn't have. I hated that Emma got the position I wanted. I let that bitterness fester, and now... look where I am."

He shook his head, his guilt pouring out. "How could God ever forgive me for that?"

Pastor Thompson's expression softened, his voice steady and calm. "God's forgiveness is boundless, Jenkins. There's nothing too dark or too deep for Him to forgive. The first step is acknowledging what you've done and being willing to turn away from it."

Jenkins wiped his face with his hands, fighting back tears. "I just don't know how to start over. I've caused so much damage. How do I even begin to make things right?"

Pastor Thompson leaned forward, his eyes full of compassion. "The fact that you want to make things right—that's where it begins.

FOUNDER'S DAY PREPARATIONS   185

God's forgiveness is waiting for you, but you also need to forgive yourself. And after that, you can start fresh. It won't be easy, but making amends, one step at a time, is how you move forward."

Jenkins took a shaky breath, the weight of his emotions pressing down on him. "I've hurt so many people. Emma... the town... I didn't think it would get this bad. I just wanted what I thought I deserved."

Pastor Thompson nodded. "We all make mistakes, Jenkins. It's what you do next that matters. You can make amends. You can turn this around. But you have to be honest—with yourself, with God, and with those you've hurt."

Jenkins' gaze dropped to the floor. "I'll testify. I know it's the right thing to do, but it doesn't make it any easier."

The pastor's voice was firm but kind. "Doing the right thing rarely is. But you've been given a chance to make things right. You can start fresh, Jenkins. And you're not alone in this."

Jenkins nodded slowly, absorbing the pastor's words. His guilt still weighed heavily, but there was a flicker of hope inside him—a glimmer of something that hadn't been there before. "I'll do it. I'll testify. And after that... I'll start making amends."

Pastor Thompson smiled gently. "One step at a time. And know that God's grace will be with you through every one of those steps."

Jenkins stood, though the burden wasn't entirely lifted, he felt a little lighter. "Thank you, Pastor. I've got a lot to think about. But maybe... maybe I can fix some of what I've broken."

"You can," Pastor Thompson said with quiet certainty. "And you will."

As Jenkins left the church, still uncertain but determined, he realized that facing the truth was his only way out. He would testify, and after that, he would begin making things right—starting with Emma.

***

The moon hung high in the night sky, casting a soft glow over the nearly finished house. Inside, the faint sound of hammers and drills echoed as Luke, Tommy, Gabe, and their dads worked late into the night. The once-dilapidated building was beginning to look like a home—a few more touches and it would be perfect.

Tom wiped his brow and leaned against the wall, grinning at his son. "This place is coming together, Luke. You've outdone yourself."

Luke barely looked up from his work, focused on installing the last section of trim. "Thanks, Dad. But it's not done yet. We've still got a lot to do before Founder's Day, and that's just the day after tomorrow."

Gabe laughed as he handed Tommy a tool. "You'd think we were rebuilding the town square itself, the way he's going at this."

Tommy chuckled, nudging Luke with his elbow. "Yeah, man, take a breather. You've been working like a machine. It's looking great."

Luke finally paused, taking a deep breath as he surveyed the progress. The walls were freshly painted, the floors sanded and polished, and the furniture they'd brought in was arranged just the way he'd imagined. It was more than a house—it was a future, a promise.

But even as he admired the work, his mind was elsewhere. "I'm glad it's coming together, but we've got to finish this on time. No room for mistakes."

Tom sensed his son's tension and placed a hand on his shoulder. "You're doing good work, son. But something tells me this isn't just about the house."

FOUNDER'S DAY PREPARATIONS

Luke exhaled slowly, setting down his hammer. "I guess... I'm just thinking about a lot of things. Kevin, for one. The way he's been acting lately—it's like he's got something up his sleeve. I don't trust him."

Tommy's smile faded as he nodded. "Yeah, I've noticed that too. The whole town feels it. And with everything happening so fast, it's hard not to worry."

Gabe leaned against the wall, folding his arms. "Well, whatever Kevin's planning, we'll be ready. You've got this project under control, Luke. Don't let him throw you off."

Luke nodded but remained quiet. His thoughts shifted to Emma. He hadn't heard from her all day, and with the pressure of Founder's Day and the ongoing tension with Kevin, he couldn't help but worry. "I'm also wondering how Emma's holding up. Haven't heard from her today."

Tom glanced over at Luke. "She's strong, Luke. She's got a lot on her plate with everything going on, but she knows how to handle it. Don't let your worry distract you."

Luke tried to smile, but the weight of everything still pressed down on him. "Yeah, I know she can handle herself. But with Kevin in the mix... I just hope she's okay."

Tom patted him on the back. "She's got you, and she's got her friends. And once this house is finished, you'll have a lot more to offer her—a real future."

Luke nodded, a glimmer of hope creeping into his thoughts. The house was almost done, and with every board nailed and every coat of paint applied, it felt like a step closer to the life he wanted. But the uncertainty lingered, and he knew that until everything with Kevin was resolved, the future was still hanging in the balance.

The group worked on, their bond growing stronger with every laugh and shared moment. There was banter and lighthearted teasing, but for Luke, the focus remained sharp. He couldn't afford to slip up—not when everything was so close to coming together.

As the night wore on, the house began to feel less like a project and more like a home. And yet, in the back of Luke's mind, the questions remained. What was Kevin up to? And would Emma be okay once everything came to a head?

Chapter Eighteen
Founder's Day Eve

EMMA WAS HUNCHED OVER her desk, focused on the endless checklists for Founder's Day. Just two days away, and she still had so much to handle. The buzzing of her phone startled her, and she glanced at the screen. **Sheriff's Office**.

Her heart skipped a beat as she answered. "This is Emma."

The sheriff's voice was steady but carried an urgency that made Emma sit up straighter. "Emma, it's Sheriff Daniels. You need to come down to the station. The FBI's in town, and they're all over Kevin. This is big."

Emma's pulse quickened. "The FBI? What's going on?"

"I'll explain everything when you get here. Just come as soon as you can. You'll want to be here for this."

Emma swallowed hard, her mind racing. "Alright, I'll be there right away."

She hung up, her fingers trembling slightly as she processed the sheriff's words. The FBI... Kevin... everything was coming to a head. She felt the weight of the situation settle over her.

Before heading out, she quickly dialed her mom. Mary picked up on the second ring.

"Hey, Mom. I need you to pray," Emma said, her voice tense but controlled.

"Of course, honey. What's going on?"

"The FBI's in town, and it sounds serious. I'm on my way to the sheriff's office now. Just... pray for me, for the town. I feel like everything's about to come to a head."

Mary's calm voice was a balm in the storm. "I'll be praying, Emma. God's got this, and so do you. You're stronger than you know."

Emma felt a rush of warmth, her mom's words grounding her. "Thanks, Mom. I'll call you later."

"Take care, sweetheart. We're all behind you."

As she hung up, Emma took a deep breath and grabbed her keys. It was time to face whatever was waiting for her at the sheriff's office.

***

Emma pushed open the heavy door of the sheriff's office, her heart racing as she stepped inside. She immediately spotted her father, Pastor Thompson, standing beside the city attorney, Mr. Wheeler. Her confusion deepened—what was her dad doing here?

Sheriff Daniels approached her, his expression serious. "Emma, thanks for coming so quickly. Let's head to the back. We've got company."

Emma followed him, her mind spinning with questions. As they entered a private room, she saw two men in dark suits—FBI agents—waiting for them. One of them stood and extended his hand.

"Mayor Thompson, I'm Agent Collins. This is Agent Moore," he said, his tone respectful. "We've been monitoring Kevin Pollard for some time now, and it looks like things are about to come to a head."

Emma's stomach churned. "Monitoring him? What's happening?"

The agent glanced at the sheriff, then back to Emma. "We've had Kevin under surveillance for weeks. We believe he's involved in illegal activities—bribery, fraud, possibly worse. We've been collecting evidence, and we're close to securing an arrest warrant, but we need the final pieces to fall into place."

Emma nodded slowly, processing the gravity of the situation. "How can I help you? We've been working on this too, on our side."

Agent Collins nodded. "I know. Your dad just filled us in about Jenkins, Linda, and Reynolds. We need them all here first thing in the morning to give their statements before we can get our arrest warrants."

Emma's eyes widened. "Reynolds? The investor?"

Agent Collins confirmed, "Yes. He's ready to cooperate, but we need all three testimonies to ensure Kevin doesn't slip through the cracks. We're putting a watch on him tonight to make sure he doesn't try to skip town."

Sheriff Daniels added, "We've got Kevin under close surveillance. If he makes any move, we'll know about it. But we need you to help make sure everything goes smoothly tomorrow."

Emma was still processing the information when she turned to her dad, Pastor Thompson. "Dad, what are you doing here?"

Pastor Thompson exchanged a glance with Mr. Wheeler before stepping forward. "Emma, Jenkins came to me for spiritual guidance a while back. He's been struggling with his choices, and I've been helping him work through things. Just like Mary has been helping Linda."

Emma's chest tightened. Her father had been helping Jenkins behind the scenes, and she hadn't known. "Why didn't you tell me?"

"I couldn't," her dad said gently. "Jenkins needed confidentiality, and I needed to keep it quiet while I prayed and supported him. I'm sorry if this hurts you, but I was doing what I felt was best."

Emma's frustration mixed with relief. She felt overwhelmed by the secrets, but also thankful that things were finally coming to light. "I just wish I'd known. But if this is what it takes to bring Kevin down, I'll support it."

Agent Collins interrupted, his voice firm. "We'll need you here tomorrow, Mayor Thompson. It's important that everything runs smoothly."

Emma nodded, her resolve strengthening. "I'll be here."

As the meeting wrapped up, Emma felt a strange mix of emotions—shock, betrayal, and hope. Kevin's time was running out, and for the first time in a long while, it felt like justice was finally within reach.

***

The parsonage was quiet, the tension palpable as the evening settled in. Jenkins sat at the dining table with Pastor Thompson, his hands trembling slightly, while Mary was down in the basement with Linda, making sure the two of them stayed out of each other's sight.

In the dimly lit dining room, Pastor Thompson leaned in closer to Jenkins, his voice calm and steady. "Jenkins, I know this isn't easy, but you're on the right path. You've come to terms with what needs to be done, and tomorrow is your chance to make things right."

Jenkins shook his head, his voice low and filled with uncertainty. "I don't know, Pastor. What if this just makes things worse? What if... what if people hate me even more for what I've done?"

Pastor Thompson's eyes softened. "Doing the right thing is never easy, Jenkins. But facing the truth will help you find peace. The truth has a way of mending things, even if it's hard to face at first."

Jenkins rubbed his temples, feeling the weight of his decisions. "I betrayed so many people in this town. I wanted power, and now I've lost everything."

Pastor Thompson placed a comforting hand on his shoulder. "You haven't lost everything. By coming forward, you'll be able to rebuild—not just your life, but your relationships. And you're not alone. We'll get through this together."

Jenkins looked up at Pastor Thompson, his eyes brimming with guilt. "I just want it to be over."

Daniel nodded, understanding. "It will be soon. Just take one step at a time. Tomorrow is the first step toward healing."

Meanwhile, down in the basement, Mary sat beside Linda, who was wrapped in a blanket, her hands still trembling from the day's events. The basement had been set up to keep Linda hidden from prying eyes, but the emotional burden she carried weighed heavily on her.

"I don't know how I'm going to get through tomorrow, Mary," Linda whispered, her voice barely above a tremble. "What if Kevin finds out what I'm doing? What if this all backfires?"

Mary reached out, gently taking Linda's hand. "You're stronger than you think, Linda. And you're doing this for the right reasons. You've already shown so much bravery just by coming forward."

Linda glanced down at her tea, still warm in her hands, her voice shaky. "I've made so many mistakes... I don't know if anyone will believe me."

"They will," Mary reassured her. "You have the truth on your side, and that's what matters. You'll find that when you speak the truth, you'll feel lighter, like a weight's been lifted."

Linda's eyes welled with tears. "I'm just so scared."

Mary gave her a warm smile. "It's okay to be scared. But you're not alone. We're all here to support you, and tomorrow, when you stand up and tell your story, you'll know that you did the right thing."

Linda took a deep breath, her resolve slowly strengthening. "You're right. I can't keep hiding. I have to face this."

Mary nodded, her voice soft but firm. "And you will. We'll get through this, one step at a time."

***

The sound of a truck backing up broke the stillness of the early evening as Luke stood outside the house, watching the final delivery of furniture and appliances arrive. The sun was beginning to set, casting a warm glow over the nearly finished home. He smiled to himself, taking in the sight of what had been a run-down building now transformed into something that felt like a real home.

The delivery guys moved swiftly, carrying in boxes and pieces of furniture that Luke had carefully selected. A couch here, a dining table there—each item placed in its perfect spot. Luke directed them with quiet satisfaction, feeling a sense of accomplishment wash over him. But beneath that satisfaction was something deeper: hope.

As the last appliance was unloaded, the building inspector arrived, clipboard in hand. "Looks like everything's coming together nicely," the inspector said, giving the house a once-over. "Ready for the final inspection?"

Luke nodded, walking alongside him as they went through the checklist. The inspector checked the wiring, the plumbing, the structure—everything was in order. Luke stood back, watching, his thoughts wandering.

It wasn't just the house. It was the future he was building in his mind. A future with Emma. As the inspector finished, Luke's heart raced with a mixture of excitement and nerves. He had been working on this house with Emma in mind the entire time, dreaming of the life they could have together.

"Everything looks good," the inspector finally said, jotting down a few notes on his clipboard. "You've got your occupancy permit. This place is ready to be lived in."

Luke smiled, a wave of relief flooding over him. "Thanks. I appreciate it."

As the inspector left, Luke stood alone in the quiet house. The furniture, the appliances, everything was in place. But the house was just a building—it was the life he imagined filling it that made his heart ache. He could picture Emma here with him, the two of them laughing, sharing meals, growing old together. It all felt so close, yet so far away.

Luke walked over to the window, looking out at the creek that ran nearby. His thoughts drifted to the past few weeks—his time back in Carter's Creek, working on the house, supporting Emma through the ordeal with Kevin. He had come back to town unsure of what he wanted, but now, it was clear. He knew what he wanted. He wanted her.

"I've lost myself in love," he whispered, a soft smile tugging at his lips.

As he stood there, alone in the home he'd built with Emma in mind, Luke allowed himself to dream—dream of the life they could have together, of the future that was just within reach. All that was left was to take that final step.

***

Kevin paced the length of his office, his nerves frayed and his mind racing. Founder's Day was looming, and nothing was going as planned. Vince was in custody, Jenkins was acting strange, and now the investors were starting to ask too many questions.

He grabbed his phone off the desk, scrolling through his contacts. His fingers hovered for a moment before he dialed. The line rang twice before a gravelly voice answered.

"Yeah?" the voice on the other end said, sounding annoyed.

Kevin's voice was tight, betraying his desperation. "I need to know where Jenkins stands. He's getting cold feet, and if he flips, we're all screwed."

There was a pause on the other end of the line before the voice replied, "Last I heard, he's still on board, but you'd better keep him close. He's unpredictable."

Kevin cursed under his breath. "Unpredictable doesn't cut it. I need him locked down. If he talks to anyone, it's over."

"Then deal with him," the voice said, a clear warning in his tone.

Kevin hung up without another word, frustration boiling over. He couldn't afford to lose control now. Not when everything was so close.

He dialed another number—one of his investors. The line picked up after several rings, and Kevin didn't bother with pleasantries. "Look, I've got everything under control. There's no reason to panic."

The investor's voice was cold. "You told us this would be wrapped up by now, Kevin. It's dragging on, and I don't like how things are looking. If you can't deliver, we're pulling out."

Kevin felt a cold sweat on his neck. "I'm telling you, it's handled. Just give me a little more time. Everything will be settled after Founder's Day."

"Time's running out," the investor replied. "Don't make us regret trusting you."

Kevin's grip on the phone tightened. "You won't. I'll fix this. You have my word."

He ended the call and tossed the phone onto his desk, running a hand through his hair. His nerves were shot, and nothing was going the way it was supposed to. He needed to regain control, but the walls were closing in faster than he could keep up.

Across town, in an unmarked van parked near Kevin's office, the FBI agents sat, headphones on, listening to every word Kevin had just said. One of them smiled grimly.

"We've got him," Agent Collins muttered, jotting down notes. "He's hanging by a thread."

***

The night air was cool and still as Emma stood at the edge of the gazebo, staring out at the quiet town. The gazebo, finally complete, stood as a symbol of all the work that had gone into Founder's Day—and maybe something more. The lights from the town square flickered in the distance, and for a moment, everything felt peaceful.

Footsteps on the wooden steps behind her made her smile. She didn't need to turn around to know it was Luke. "It's beautiful, isn't it?" she said softly, her voice carrying in the quiet night.

Luke joined her, his hands resting on the railing. "Yeah, it is. They did a good job."

Emma glanced at him with a knowing smile. "You did a good job."

Luke shrugged, a small smile tugging at his lips. "I had a little help."

For a moment, they stood in silence, just the two of them and the gazebo they'd known since childhood. Emma's eyes drifted down to a familiar spot on one of the posts, and there it was—their initials, still carved into the wood after all these years.

"I can't believe our initials are still here," Emma said, tracing the worn marks with her fingers. "It feels like we've come full circle."

Luke chuckled, his voice warm. "Maybe it's a sign that we're right where we're supposed to be."

Emma sighed, leaning against the railing. "Maybe."

Luke studied her for a moment, noticing the way she seemed both calm and on edge. "You okay?" he asked.

Emma hesitated, her mind swirling with everything she couldn't say. She glanced at him, a soft smile playing on her lips. "I think… everything's going to be resolved tomorrow," she said carefully, choosing her words. "I can't say much more than that, but… things are going to change."

Luke's heart raced, and his thoughts immediately went to the house. Did she know? Had someone told her about what he'd been planning all along? "Resolved?" he asked, trying to sound casual. "What kind of resolution are we talking about?"

Emma's smile widened, though she still kept her secret. "Just… something big. Something that's been hanging over us for a while. You'll see."

Luke nodded, his mind torn between what she might know about Kevin and the growing hope that she'd somehow found out about the house. "I'll hold you to that," he said lightly, though his curiosity was piqued.

They stood in comfortable silence for a few more minutes, the weight of the night lingering between them. The gazebo, the town, everything felt like it was on the brink of change—and neither of them knew exactly what the next day would bring.

As they finally said their goodbyes, walking in opposite directions, Luke couldn't shake the feeling that tomorrow would change everything—for better or for worse.

Chapter Nineteen
Founder's Day Event Begins

THE SUN BEAMED DOWN on Carter's Creek as the Founder's Day Parade wound its way through the town. Children waved flags, vendors sold cotton candy and ice cream, and the festive energy was contagious. At the head of the parade, Emma led with grace as mayor, Luke by her side, the perfect picture of hometown pride.

But off to the side, under a shaded canopy near the square, a group of town gossips gathered, their eyes keenly tracking the scene unfolding before them. Their voices were hushed but brimming with curiosity.

"Look at her," one whispered, nodding toward Emma. "Hasn't fallen for a man in years, and now she's walking around town with Luke Hunter like it's nothing."

Another leaned in, squinting in the sun. "Do you really think this time it'll be different? She's always been too busy for love. I mean, running this town? There's no time for romance."

The older woman of the group smirked. "Emma's got walls as high as this town's hills. Luke's a good man, but she's never needed one before—why start now?"

The second woman shrugged. "Maybe. But have you heard what Luke's been doing out at the creek? They're saying he's been working on something big. You know how close he and Emma used to be. Could be he's trying to win her over."

The first woman scoffed, but her eyes lingered on Luke. "We've tried to keep it a secret, but... well, you know how things spread in Carter's Creek."

They all chuckled knowingly, before the conversation shifted to more pressing town gossip.

"And speaking of men, what about Kevin Pollard?" one of them chimed in, her voice lowering as if Kevin himself might overhear. "I heard he's in deep trouble with the law."

The third woman leaned in conspiratorially. "Oh, he's in trouble all right. Rumor has it the FBI's been sniffing around. People are saying Kevin might be headed out of town on a rail before this whole thing blows up in his face."

The second woman snorted. "Good riddance. That man's been nothing but a headache since he got here."

The older woman nodded. "Well, we'll see. If he's got any sense left, he'll high-tail it before the parade's even over. Otherwise, it'll be too late."

As the parade marched on, the gossips exchanged glances, splitting their attention between Emma and Luke's undeniable connection and the whispers of Kevin's impending downfall. There was tension in the air, and they could all feel that something big was on the horizon for Carter's Creek.

FOUNDER'S DAY EVENT BEGINS 203

***

The sheriff's office was buzzing with quiet tension as Linda, Jenkins, and Reynolds sat separately, waiting their turn to testify. One by one, they were called into the room, each carrying their own set of fears, hopes, and burdens.

Linda was the first to testify. She took her seat across from Agent Collins, her hands trembling slightly as she began to recount her role in Kevin's dealings. At first, her voice was soft, wavering with uncertainty, but as she spoke, her confidence grew.

"I didn't realize what I was getting into at first," Linda admitted, her eyes darting between the FBI agents. "But once I was in, it was too late. Kevin... he made it clear there was no way out."

She took a deep breath, her eyes flicking toward Mary, who was sitting nearby for support. "But I'm done being afraid. This is my chance to make things right."

When she finished, Linda felt an unexpected sense of relief wash over her. The weight she had carried for so long seemed to lift from her shoulders. As she stood up, she turned to Mary, her eyes glistening. "I think I'm ready to turn the corner now. I've got people in my life who care about me, and I never thought I'd have that."

Mary smiled warmly and pulled Linda into a comforting hug. "You're not alone anymore, Linda. You've got us."

For the first time in a long time, Linda believed it.

Next came Jenkins, accompanied by Pastor Thompson, whose presence steadied him as he walked into the room. His heart raced, and his hands were clammy as he sat down. His mind whirled with guilt and fear, but he had made his decision—he was going to finish what he'd started.

Agent Collins gave him a sharp look. "Remember, Mr. Jenkins, if your statement isn't completely truthful, you will lose the immunity deal we've discussed. We need everything—the full truth. No holding back."

Jenkins nodded, swallowing hard. "I understand."

He cleared his throat and began his testimony, his voice shaky at first. "I... I believed Kevin when he said there would be no risks. I thought it was all for the good of the town. I pushed through the permits, thinking it was harmless. But I was wrong."

Jenkins hesitated, looking to Pastor Thompson, who gave him a reassuring nod. "The truth is, I did it for myself too. I wanted the power, the status. But it's all fallen apart, and now I have to make it right."

Agent Collins leaned forward. "What else? We need the full picture, Jenkins."

Jenkins swallowed hard again, his voice breaking slightly. "When the council started asking questions, and Linda disappeared... I realized that everything Kevin promised was a lie. I can't live with that anymore."

When Jenkins finished, he felt drained but resolute. He wasn't sure what would come next, but for the first time in months, he felt like he could face whatever was coming with his head held high.

As he stood to leave, Pastor Thompson patted him on the back. "You did the right thing, Jenkins. You've taken the first step toward healing."

Jenkins gave a small nod. "I just want to finish strong."

Reynolds, the investor, followed, his demeanor markedly different from the others. He walked into the room with an air of quiet confidence, his expression calm and collected. He sat down and immediately began his testimony with a straightforward tone.

FOUNDER'S DAY EVENT BEGINS

"Kevin lied to me and the other investors. He promised us a solid, foolproof plan, but it was all smoke and mirrors. The money we put in has gone to places it never should have, and I want to see him held accountable for it."

Reynolds' testimony was clear, direct, and efficient. There were no lingering doubts in his mind—he wanted justice for the people Kevin had deceived.

When he finished, Reynolds stood and shook hands with Agent Collins. "I hope this brings an end to Kevin's schemes. The town deserves better."

As Reynolds walked out of the room, there was a sense of finality in his steps. He was hopeful that with the truth laid bare, the town could begin to heal from the damage Kevin had caused.

***

Kevin Pollard sat in his office, the blinds half-closed, casting long shadows over his desk. The sound of the Founder's Day celebrations filtered through the open window, but Kevin wasn't in a festive mood. Sweat beaded on his forehead as he paced back and forth, his mind racing.

Vince had been arrested. Jenkins was acting shifty. And now, his investors were starting to get anxious. Kevin knew he had to act fast before everything unraveled. If he didn't control the situation now, he'd be done for—his empire would crumble, and there'd be nothing left.

Grabbing his phone off the desk, Kevin scrolled through his contacts and found the number he was looking for. He dialed quickly, his hands shaking. The line rang once, twice, and then a gruff voice answered.

"Yeah?"

Kevin cleared his throat, forcing calm into his voice. "I need you to do something for me. It's... delicate."

The voice on the other end grunted. "What kind of delicate are we talking about?"

Kevin's jaw tightened. "I need someone taken out of the equation—just for a few hours. Keep her out of sight long enough for me to handle the rest."

"Her?" the voice asked, curiosity piqued.

"Mayor Thompson," Kevin said, his voice barely above a whisper. "She's sticking her nose in where it doesn't belong. Get her out of the way, and I'll make it worth your while."

There was a brief pause on the other end of the line, then the voice chuckled. "You're asking a lot, Pollard. You sure you want to go down this road?"

Kevin's grip on the phone tightened. "I don't have a choice. You take care of her, and I'll make sure you're paid handsomely."

The man on the other end hummed thoughtfully. "All right. I'll take care of it. You'll get your results."

Kevin let out a breath he didn't realize he'd been holding. "Good. Don't screw this up."

He ended the call and tossed the phone onto his desk, staring out the window as the sounds of the town's celebration grew louder. He knew he was playing a dangerous game, but it was the only way to buy himself more time.

Across town, in an unmarked car parked near Kevin's office, an undercover FBI agent sat, headphones on, listening to every word. He smiled grimly as he jotted down notes.

"Gotcha," the agent muttered under his breath. He picked up his radio and spoke into it. "Pollard just made the call. He's trying to bribe someone to take out Mayor Thompson. We've got all the evidence we need."

Kevin believed he was making his last-ditch effort to save himself, unaware that every word was being monitored by the FBI. The net was closing in.

***

The makeshift FBI headquarters in Carter's Creek was buzzing with quiet urgency. Agent Collins stood in front of a large map of the town, flanked by a small team of agents who had been working around the clock. The atmosphere was thick with anticipation—they were closing in on Kevin Pollard, and today was the day they would make their move.

Collins nodded toward one of the agents monitoring a recording device. "We have everything we need. Kevin's desperate. The call he made about Mayor Thompson just sealed the deal."

The agent played back the recording briefly, the sound of Kevin's voice as he tried to arrange Emma's kidnapping filling the room. Collins' jaw tightened as he listened. "That's the final nail in the coffin."

One of the other agents looked up from his notes. "Do we have the warrant ready?"

Collins nodded. "We do. We've got the statements from Jenkins, Linda, and Reynolds. Now, with this phone call, we've got enough to arrest him."

The team gathered around the map as Collins continued. "Kevin's been trying to keep his plans intact, but he's slipping. We've got eyes on him, and we'll make our move once he's at the parade. We can't risk him skipping town."

Another agent chimed in, "We've alerted local law enforcement. They're ready to assist if Kevin tries to make a run for it."

Collins turned to the group, his expression serious. "The arrest warrant is ready. We're going to wait until he's in a public place, so there's no way he can escape without drawing attention. Founder's Day is the perfect opportunity. He'll be too distracted trying to make his last-ditch effort to save himself."

The team nodded in agreement. The plan was set in motion, and now it was just a matter of timing.

As the team made their final preparations, Collins glanced at the clock. The parade was well underway, and soon Kevin would show his face. The FBI had everything in place, and by the end of the day, Kevin Pollard would be in handcuffs.

Back in town, the celebration was still in full swing, with people unaware of the storm brewing just beneath the surface. But for Agent Collins and his team, the day's festivities were merely the backdrop to the biggest takedown Carter's Creek had ever seen.

***

The Founder's Day Parade was still in full swing, but as Emma and Luke neared the end of the parade route, a sense of unease crept over them. The day had gone smoothly so far, but both could feel something looming.

FOUNDER'S DAY EVENT BEGINS

Emma slowed her pace, casting a worried glance at Luke. "I can't shake the feeling that something's about to go wrong."

Luke scanned the crowd, his brow furrowed. "Yeah, it's like we're just waiting for it."

They approached the stage, where Emma was set to give her mid-day speech as mayor, with Luke by her side. The crowd was cheering, the sun was shining, but beneath it all, something felt off. Emma's mind raced, thoughts of Kevin, the town, and everything hanging in the balance swirling through her head.

Emma took a deep breath, squeezing Luke's hand as they reached the base of the stage. "I just need to know that no matter what happens, you'll be with me."

Luke turned to face her, his expression serious but full of reassurance. "I'm not going anywhere. We're in this together. Whatever happens next, I've got your back."

Emma gave him a small smile, though her heart still felt heavy. "Okay... we've got this."

As they turned to step onto the stage, the crowd's applause filled the square. The town had gathered in anticipation of Emma's speech, eager to hear their mayor address the day's festivities. But as they ascended the steps, something caught both Emma and Luke's attention.

From across the square, Kevin Pollard was approaching, moving through the crowd with a purposeful stride. His presence, dark and imposing, sent a shiver down Emma's spine. Luke noticed it too, his jaw tightening as Kevin neared the stage.

Emma's heart skipped a beat. This was it. Whatever Kevin had planned, it was about to unfold.

They exchanged a glance, a silent agreement passing between them—stay strong, stay together, no matter what this day held.

As they reached the top of the stage, Kevin came closer, and the tension between them all was palpable. The next moments would change everything.

Chapter Twenty
Confrontation on Founder's Day

EMMA AND LUKE ASCENDED the steps to the stage, the cheers from the crowd swelling around them. But as they neared the podium, Emma's steps faltered. From the corner of her eye, she saw Kevin pushing through the crowd, his eyes locked on her.

She froze for a moment, her heart hammering in her chest. "Luke... Kevin's here."

Luke followed her gaze, spotting Kevin moving closer, his stride purposeful. "I see him," he muttered, tensing beside her. "Stay calm."

Emma's breath caught, the tension between them and Kevin thickening with each step he took. The celebrations were still in full swing, oblivious to what was about to unfold.

"Is he going to try something?" Emma whispered, worry creeping into her voice.

Luke stood protectively next to her, his hand gently brushing hers in reassurance, nodding to his left. "Not if the FBI gets to him first."

As Kevin moved closer, his expression dark and calculating, two figures stepped into his path—Agent Collins and another FBI agent. Kevin barely had time to react before Agent Collins flashed his badge.

"Kevin Pollard," Agent Collins called out, loud enough for those nearby to hear, "you're under arrest for conspiracy, bribery, and fraud."

Immediately, local police officers moved in, clearing the crowd and creating a circle of safe distance around the scene. The mood shifted from festive to tense as people were ushered back, giving the FBI and police space to act.

Kevin's face twisted in disbelief. "You can't do this! Not here!" he shouted, attempting to push through the agents, but Collins was quicker. Grabbing Kevin's arm, he twisted it behind his back, snapping the handcuffs into place.

The crowd fell silent, murmurs spreading as they watched the scene unfold. The FBI agents moved with precision, showing no hesitation as they took Kevin into custody.

"You have the right to remain silent," Agent Collins began, his voice calm but firm. "Anything you say can and will be used against you in a court of law. You have the right to an attorney..."

Kevin's defiant expression faltered as the reality of the situation sank in. The Miranda rights echoed through the air, mixing with the shocked gasps of the crowd.

As the FBI led Kevin away in handcuffs, more police officers maintained the barrier, ensuring the townspeople kept their distance. Whispers rippled through the crowd, and the tension was palpable. Some exchanged stunned looks, while others murmured about the justice finally being served.

From the edge of the stage, Emma and Luke stood side by side, watching as Kevin was escorted through the throngs of people.

CONFRONTATION ON FOUNDER'S DAY 213

Emma's heart raced, the enormity of the moment hitting her all at once.

"It's really happening," Emma whispered, her eyes wide as she watched Kevin disappear from view.

Luke, standing close by, nodded. "It's over, Emma. He's done."

The tension that had gripped Carter's Creek began to dissolve, replaced by a wave of relief and jubilation. The police officers gave a nod of confirmation, signaling that the area was secure, and gradually pulled back, allowing the townspeople to reassemble near the stage.

Emma stood at the edge of the platform, her heart still racing from the intensity of the day's events. As she stepped forward to address the crowd, a lingering thought tugged at her mind: **Why wasn't Jenkins arrested too?** She caught a glimpse of him standing with her parents and Linda, clearly relaxed with a huge smile. The sight puzzled her, but there was nothing she could do about it now—justice would come in time.

Shaking off the thought, Emma approached the microphone. As soon as she appeared, the townspeople erupted into cheers, louder and more enthusiastic than she had anticipated. Her smile brightened as she took in the sight of her community—her people—cheering together after such a tumultuous time.

Raising her arms to quiet them, Emma's voice echoed across the square. "Thank you," she began, her heart swelling with pride. "Thank you, everyone. Today, we celebrate more than just Founder's Day—we celebrate the strength, resilience, and unity of Carter's Creek."

Her eyes found Linda, Jenkins, and Reynolds standing near the front. Seeing them there, part of this moment, meant everything. Their courage had been vital in taking Kevin down, even if Jenkins' fate still hung in the balance.

Off to the side, a group of the town's most notorious gossips exchanged knowing glances. Emma couldn't help but overhear their whispers as she paused.

"We knew it," one of them said with a self-satisfied grin. "Nothing gets by us."

"Of course," another agreed. "Kevin thought he could pull a fast one, but not in Carter's Creek."

Emma suppressed a small chuckle, amused by the familiar banter. It was part of the town's charm—everyone had their ear to the ground, and nothing stayed hidden for long.

Turning back to the microphone, Emma spotted Luke standing quietly at the edge of the stage, his hands tucked into his pockets, watching her with a calm smile. Gratitude bloomed in her chest. If anyone had been her anchor through all of this, it was him.

"And a special thank you to Luke Hunter," Emma continued, her voice warm and sincere. "For taking the time to restore our beloved gazebo. It's been a symbol of this town for so long, and now, thanks to Luke, it will continue to be part of our history for generations to come."

The crowd burst into applause again. Luke, ever humble, gave a small nod, raising one hand in a modest wave to acknowledge the cheers. His quiet determination had meant so much to her and the town.

As the applause subsided, Emma gestured to the table set up beside the stage. Awards waited, shining brightly in the afternoon sun.

"And now," Emma announced, a playful lightness entering her voice, "it's time to recognize some of the incredible talent we've seen today. First up, let's give a big round of applause to our Best Band—Carter's Creek High School Band! They win every year, and this year was no different. Their performance really set the tone for today's celebration."

The band members grinned widely as they made their way to the stage, accepting their award to the sound of the town's cheers. Emma smiled as she handed over the prize, the joy on their faces infectious.

"And of course," she continued, "the Best Float Award goes to Sadie's Sweet Rolls! Your creativity and dedication brought the parade to life today. Your float was a true masterpiece."

Sadie, standing proudly with her team, made her way to the stage, her face lighting up in surprise and joy as Emma handed her the award. "Thank you so much," Sadie said, giving Emma a heartfelt hug. "We put a lot of love into it, and I'm thrilled that everyone enjoyed it."

As the excitement died down once more, Emma turned back to the microphone with one final announcement. "Thank you all for making today so special. And don't forget—we're not done yet! I invite everyone back here tonight for the Founder's Day Party in the Square. There will be food, music, dancing, and plenty of fun. Let's celebrate what makes Carter's Creek truly remarkable—each other."

The crowd erupted once more, the energy contagious as the townspeople clapped and cheered. The dark cloud that had loomed over Carter's Creek for so long had finally lifted, and now, they could free themselves to celebrate the joy of being together.

Emma stepped back from the microphone, catching Luke's eye once more. As the crowd around them buzzed with excitement for the evening to come, she felt a deep sense of peace settle over her. Despite her confusion about Jenkins, there was a new clarity in her mind. The town was safe again, and tonight, they would celebrate all that they had built together.

***

As the sun dipped lower, casting a warm glow over the square, the energy of the town shifted from the day's formalities to a night of celebration. People streamed in from all corners of Carter's Creek, gathering for the long-awaited Founder's Day Party. The band tuned their instruments, the lights around the square flickered to life, and the air buzzed with excitement.

Emma stood with Sadie and Hannah, admiring one another's outfits, their laughter bubbling over as they reminisced about the day's events. Emma smoothed down the simple but elegant dress she had changed into, glancing around at the lively atmosphere. Her heart felt light—finally, there was room for joy after everything that had happened.

Sadie grinned, adjusting her hair. "Can you believe it? Best Float! I'm still in shock."

Hannah laughed, nudging Emma playfully. "And Emma, I swear, you were like a queen up there on that stage. Everyone was hanging on your every word."

Emma's cheeks flushed at the compliment, but her smile grew wider. "I don't know about that. It just felt so good to see everyone happy, you know? After everything we've been through."

The girls exchanged knowing looks before bursting into giggles again, the excitement of the night filling them with energy.

Meanwhile, across the square, the guys had gathered near the front of the tavern, catching up and talking in low tones. Luke stood with Tommy and Gabe, hands in his pockets, but his eyes kept drifting toward Emma. He couldn't take his eyes off her—there was something about tonight, about everything they had been through, that made him feel more certain than ever.

CONFRONTATION ON FOUNDER'S DAY

"You going to just stare at her all night or finally make your move?" Tommy teased, elbowing Luke.

Luke chuckled, shaking his head. "Yeah, yeah. I'm getting there."

But before heading toward the girls, Luke made a quick detour. He crossed the square, weaving through the crowd until he reached the band. The leader looked up as Luke approached, curiosity in his eyes.

Luke leaned in, whispering something quietly, palming the band leader a bit of cash with a grin. The band leader nodded, a knowing smile spreading across his face, and within seconds, they started playing the opening chords of a familiar tune.

Emma's ears perked up as soon as the first notes filled the air. Her breath caught in her chest. "I Can Love You Like That." It was one of her favorite songs when she was a teenager—a song that had always held a special place in her heart.

She turned, her eyes widening in surprise as she spotted Luke walking straight toward her, that easy, confident smile on his face. He came to a stop right in front of her, offering his hand.

"Dance with me?" Luke asked, his voice low and warm.

Emma's heart fluttered. She glanced at her friends, who were grinning at her like schoolgirls, before turning back to Luke with a soft smile. "Of course."

Luke took her hand, gently pulling her toward the center of the square as the band played. The soft, romantic melody of the song surrounded them as they moved together, swaying to the music. The world around them seemed to disappear—there was no crowd, no noise, just the two of them and the quiet intimacy of the dance.

Luke's arms tightened slightly around her waist, pulling her closer. Emma rested her head against his shoulder, letting herself melt into the moment. There was a familiarity in his embrace that felt like home, like something she had always known but had somehow forgotten.

The song played on, the lyrics filling the air, and Emma felt her heart swell. Luke's hand brushed against hers, his thumb gently stroking her fingers as they swayed.

As the song neared its end, Luke leaned down, his voice soft and intimate. "I've been working on something. Something I think you'll like."

Emma pulled back just enough to look up at him, her eyes filled with curiosity. "What is it?"

Luke smiled, his expression gentle but full of anticipation. "Come with me. I want to show you."

Emma's heart raced, her curiosity piqued. She nodded, her trust in him unwavering. "Okay. Show me."

With one final glance around the square, they stepped away from the dance floor, hand in hand, heading toward whatever surprise Luke had been working on. The night was just beginning, and it felt like the start of something beautiful.

Chapter Twenty-One
A Surprise and A Proposal

THE MUSIC FROM THE Founder's Day Dance still lingered in the air as Emma and Luke made their way through the bustling crowd, their hands intertwined. The evening was alive with laughter, chatter, and the soft glow of string lights that adorned the square. As they approached the exit, a familiar voice called out, cutting through the festivities.

"Emma! Luke!"

They turned to see Jenkins and Daniel walking toward them, their expressions a mix of hesitation and determination. Jenkins stepped forward first, his usual confident demeanor softened by the gravity of the moment.

"Can we talk for a moment?" Jenkins asked, his eyes meeting Emma's with sincerity.

Daniel offered an encouraging smile, his gaze shifting between Jenkins and Emma. He gave Jenkins a subtle nod, signaling his support.

Emma glanced between the two men, sensing the importance of what Jenkins was about to say. "Of course," she replied, guiding Luke to a quieter corner away from the main crowd.

Jenkins took a deep breath, the weight of his decision evident in his posture. "Emma, I need to apologize," he began, his voice steady but filled with emotion. "I've made mistakes, and I let Kevin drag me into things I shouldn't have been a part of. It's not fair to you, to the town."

Emma felt a pang of hurt but also relief. "Jenkins, I appreciate your honesty. It takes a lot to admit when you're wrong."

He nodded, taking another step closer. "I've decided to resign from the town council. I want to give back to Carter's Creek in a different way, something positive. I'm not entirely sure what that will be yet, but I promise I'm going to figure it out."

Emma reached out, pulling him into a heartfelt hug. "Thank you for taking responsibility. We all make mistakes, but what matters is that you're choosing to make things right."

Jenkins held her tightly for a moment longer before releasing her. "I'm sorry for everything, Emma."

Emma smiled, her eyes meeting his with genuine forgiveness. "It's okay, Jenkins. We're moving forward now."

She glanced back at Luke, who stood patiently by her side. "Excuse us," she said gently, turning to Jenkins and Daniel. "Luke has something to show me."

Daniel's eyes lit up as he nodded at Luke, giving him a silent blessing. "Take care, Emma. We're here if you need anything."

With a final wave, Jenkins and Daniel walked away, leaving Emma and Luke alone once more. Emma took a deep breath, feeling a sense of closure she hadn't realized she needed.

***

A SURPRISE AND A PROPOSAL

The soft glow of the porch light greeted them as Luke led Emma down the familiar path toward the house by the creek. The light from a few windows spilled out into the evening, giving the place a warm, lived-in feeling—almost as if a family was inside, waiting for their return. Emma slowed her steps, her brow furrowing in confusion. She hadn't been here in years, and now, seeing the house lit up, it stirred memories she wasn't prepared for.

"This is..." Emma trailed off, glancing at Luke, trying to make sense of it. "Why are we here, Luke?"

Luke hesitated, his hands in his pockets, feeling the weight of the moment pressing down on him. He had rehearsed this in his head, but now that it was real—now that he was standing here with her—it felt harder than ever to explain.

"I wanted to show you something," he started, but the words weren't coming out right. He could see the confusion in her eyes, and it made him stumble over the explanation. "It's... I mean... it's not like what you're probably thinking. I just..."

Emma tilted her head, her confusion deepening. "Luke, what is this? Why is this house lit up like someone's living here?"

Luke ran a hand through his hair, exhaling sharply. He had hoped this would be easier. "I didn't want to tell you until it was done, but—" He stopped, frustration building as the words kept slipping away from him. "I'm not doing this right."

Emma crossed her arms, her heart racing. There was something in his voice, in the way he was acting, that made her anxious. "Luke, you're not making any sense."

Luke took a deep breath, stepping closer to her, his voice softer now. "I love you, Emma. I always have."

The words hung in the air between them, and Emma blinked, caught off guard. The declaration wasn't what she expected, and hearing it after all these years hit her harder than she imagined. She wasn't sure how to respond—there were too many questions swirling in her mind, too much history between them.

"I don't know what to say," she whispered, her voice barely audible. "It's been so long... and I don't even know what's happening here."

Luke could see the hesitation in her eyes, the doubt creeping in, and it made him realize he needed to explain everything, and fast. He took a step back, motioning toward the house. "Do you remember when we were teenagers? We used to walk by this place and talk about living here someday."

Emma's eyes widened, the memories flooding back. She remembered those walks, those long, hopeful conversations about their future, back when life seemed so much simpler.

"When I came back to town," Luke continued, his voice steadying, "I bought it. This house. It needed a lot of work—more than I could handle on my own. That's what I've been doing all this time. Tommy and Gabe helped me finish it, and my dad and yours... they pitched in too."

Emma's mouth fell open in shock as she turned to look at the house again, now seeing it with new eyes. The light in the windows, the porch... everything started to make sense. "You... bought this place? You've been working on it?"

Luke nodded. "For us. I know I should have told you sooner, but I wanted it to be perfect before I showed you. This place... it's always been part of our story."

Emma's heart raced, and her hands trembled slightly. She wasn't sure what to say or how to process all of it. The house, Luke's words, their past—it was all coming back to her in a rush.

"Luke... I don't even know what to say," she whispered, her voice cracking slightly.

A SURPRISE AND A PROPOSAL 223

"You don't have to say anything," Luke said gently. "I just wanted you to see it. To see what I've been working on for us."

***

Emma followed Luke into the house, her steps slow as she took it all in. The house had changed since the last time they'd passed by as teenagers, but the feeling—the memory of their dreams—remained intact. Each room they entered was filled with traces of the love and care Luke had poured into making it their home.

"This is incredible," Emma whispered as they walked through the cozy living room. The walls were freshly painted, the furniture simple yet elegant, and everything seemed to radiate warmth. She could almost picture herself living here, sharing a life with Luke.

"Do you remember this?" Luke asked, leading her toward the kitchen. "We used to talk about how we'd have a big kitchen—where you could bake, and I'd try to help, but mostly just get in your way."

Emma laughed softly, nodding. "I remember. You always said you'd wash the dishes if I did the cooking."

Luke grinned, the memory bringing a twinkle to his eyes. "Well, that deal still stands."

They moved through the house, the conversation shifting to the little moments they had shared when they were younger, their dreams of a future together starting to take shape in the very walls of this home. As they finished the tour, they stepped out onto the front porch again, the night air cool and refreshing.

The soft glow of the porch light illuminated them as they stood together, the creek flowing gently in the background. Emma felt her heart swell with emotion. Everything about this moment felt right—like all the pieces of their lives had finally fallen into place.

Luke turned to face her, his expression serious but filled with love. He reached into his pocket and pulled out a small velvet box, and for a moment, Emma's breath caught in her throat.

"Emma," Luke said quietly, his voice filled with emotion. "I've loved you for as long as I can remember. And I know it hasn't always been easy, but being here with you—building this house, our dreams—has been the best part of my life. I want to spend the rest of my life with you."

Emma's eyes widened as Luke opened the box, revealing a stunning princess-cut diamond engagement ring. The light from the porch reflected off the diamond, casting tiny rainbows across the porch.

"Will you marry me?" Luke asked, his voice soft but steady.

Emma's heart pounded in her chest, her eyes filling with tears of joy. There was no hesitation, no doubt. She knew her answer.

"Yes!" she said, her voice trembling with excitement. "Yes, Luke, I will!"

Luke slipped the ring onto her finger, and without wasting another second, he pulled her into his arms, kissing her deeply. The world around them faded as they shared that perfect, long-awaited moment. Emma wrapped her arms around his neck, her heart soaring as they kissed.

The sound of cheering broke the quiet, and Emma and Luke pulled apart, both laughing as they turned to see their friends and family pouring in from the trees and paths nearby. Sadie, Hannah, Tommy, Gabe, Mary, Daniel, and Tom were all there, grinning from ear to ear.

"We knew it!" Sadie shouted, holding up her phone to snap a picture of the moment.

A SURPRISE AND A PROPOSAL 225

Hannah ran over, wrapping Emma in a tight hug. "I'm so happy for you!" she squealed, tears of joy in her eyes.

The group gathered around, taking turns congratulating them, but through it all, Emma never let go of Luke's hand. His fingers stayed tightly intertwined with hers, and though they were surrounded by love and excitement, it was clear that Luke only had eyes for her.

Tom clapped his son on the back, beaming with pride. "About time, son," he teased, though there was a softness in his voice that showed how much the moment meant to him.

Mary embraced her daughter, her eyes brimming with emotion. "You deserve all the happiness in the world, Emma," she whispered, holding her close.

Emma smiled, her heart full as she looked around at the people who meant the most to her. But even as the celebration continued, her focus remained on Luke. He was her home, her future, and she couldn't wait to start this new chapter of their lives together.

As the evening air grew cooler, Emma glanced down at her engagement ring, the diamonds sparkling in the soft light. She squeezed Luke's hand, her heart overflowing with happiness. They had come so far, and now, standing together on the porch of their dream home, everything felt exactly as it should.

Chapter Twenty-Two
A Carter's Creek Wedding

EMMA AND LUKE SAT around the cozy kitchen table, joined by Mary, Daniel, and Tom. The remnants of coffee cups and light snacks sat between them, but the conversation had taken a more serious turn.

"We've been thinking," Emma began, her fingers lightly brushing over Luke's as she spoke. "We don't want anything too fancy. Just something simple... but with enough room for everyone."

Tom leaned back in his chair, crossing his arms with a knowing grin. "Simple, huh? Doesn't sound like any woman I've ever met."

Luke nodded. "We've been through a lot lately, and we don't want to drag it out. We'd love to get married this week if we can pull it off."

Daniel exchanged a glance with Tom, both of them smiling knowingly. "The town square," Daniel said, his voice firm and certain. "It's the perfect place for an event like this. It's right in the heart of Carter's Creek, and most of the décor from Founder's Day is still up. We can reuse it—no need to start from scratch."

Emma's eyes widened, and she turned to Luke with a smile. "That's actually perfect. It's where everything's been happening lately. It feels right."

Mary, who had been listening quietly, chimed in with a determined tone. "Leave the food to me and the ladies. We'll pull together a feast for everyone. And don't worry about the cake—Sadie's Sweet Rolls will take care of that."

Emma felt a wave of relief wash over her. "Thank you, Mom. That's such a big help."

"And one more thing," Mary continued, smiling warmly. "You might not know this yet, but Linda is now working as the parsonage assistant, and she's also taken on the role of the church's newly appointed event coordinator. She can handle all the details for you, from the decorations to the seating. I think she'll do a fantastic job."

Emma blinked in surprise. "Linda's the event coordinator?"

Mary nodded. "She's doing a wonderful job already, and this will be her first big event. She's eager to prove herself, and I think she's just what you need."

Luke leaned forward, resting his elbows on the table. "That sounds perfect. I'm sure Linda will do great."

Emma smiled, feeling a weight lift from her shoulders. Everything was falling into place. "This sounds like a dream come true. I was worried about how we'd manage everything so quickly, but you've all come up with the perfect solution."

Mary reached across the table, squeezing Emma's hand. "You deserve it. And don't worry about a thing. We'll take care of all the details."

Emma nodded, feeling a surge of gratitude. "I just have a few things I need to wrap up for the town—there are still a lot of loose ends from Kevin's arrest, Jenkins' resignation, and everything else that's been happening. But I'll get it all done. I promise I'll be ready to walk down that aisle."

Tom chuckled, giving Luke a playful nudge. "Looks like you've got yourself a determined bride there."

Luke grinned, squeezing Emma's hand. "I wouldn't have it any other way."

***

The golden glow of the setting sun bathed Carter's Creek in a warm light as the town prepared for a wedding that would mark the beginning of something beautiful. In the bridal suite, Emma stood before the mirror, her heart fluttering as the final rays of sunlight streamed through the windows, casting a soft glow on her gown. The dress, the same one her mother had donned at her parents' wedding—a timeless, elegant dress that symbolized generations of love and commitment. Sadie and Hannah, her two closest friends, flitted around her, adjusting straps and smoothing out fabric, their laughter filling the room with joy.

"Alright, ladies," Linda called from the doorway, her clipboard in hand. "It's time. Let's get you all lined up."

Sadie and Hannah exchanged excited glances before turning to Emma. "You look stunning, Em," Sadie said, her eyes sparkling with happiness.

"Yeah, you really do," Hannah added, giving Emma's shoulder a reassuring squeeze.

As her friends moved toward the door, Mary quietly entered the room, holding Emma's veil delicately. She moved gracefully, slipping into the bridal suite and approaching Emma with a gentle smile.

"Come here, sweetheart," Mary whispered, her voice soft yet filled with emotion. She placed the veil over Emma's head, her hands steady and loving. "You look beautiful."

Emma felt a lump form in her throat as her mother's words washed over her. "Thank you, Mom."

Mary took Emma's hands in hers, her eyes filled with wisdom and love. "Emma, marriage is hard. It's beautiful and full of love, but it's hard sometimes. The most important thing is to never quit. No matter what happens, never give up on each other. Always make up, even when it feels difficult."

Emma nodded, tears welling up in her eyes. "I promise, Mom. I'll never quit."

Mary gave her daughter a tight hug, her heart swelling with pride. "You're going to be an amazing wife. And Luke... he's a good man."

As the heartfelt moment lingered, Linda reappeared, her enthusiasm returning. "Alright, Emma! Time to line up behind your friends."

Sadie and Hannah were already in line, glancing back to give Emma one last encouraging smile. Emma took a deep breath, her heart racing with a mixture of excitement and nerves. This was the moment she had dreamed of her entire life.

Meanwhile, in the groom's room, Luke stood with Tommy and Gabe, adjusting his tie for the tenth time that morning. His nerves were starting to show, but he was more than ready for this day. Tommy leaned in, giving him a playful nudge.

"You still have time to escape if you've changed your mind," Tommy teased, eliciting a round of laughter from the guys.

Gabe chuckled, clapping Luke on the back. "Yeah, don't worry. We've got your back."

The laughter helped relieve the tension Luke felt, a reminder that he wasn't alone. He took a deep breath, feeling the support of his friends. "I've never been more sure of anything in my life!"

Luke smiled, his confidence growing as he prepared to take the next step. Linda entered the room once more, clipboard in hand, and addressed the guys. "Alright, gentlemen. Time to line up in front."

Tommy and Gabe exchanged knowing glances before moving to their designated spots. Luke was the last to step forward, but before he could leave, Tom slipped in beside him, walking step-for-step with his son.

"Luke," Tom began, his voice filled with pride, "I just wanted to tell you how proud I am of you. You've grown into the kind of man I always hoped you'd be."

Luke felt a lump form in his throat, touched by his father's words. "Thanks, Dad."

Tom placed a reassuring hand on Luke's shoulder. "Always love and cherish Emma. When you do that every day, you remember how important she is to your life."

Luke nodded, his heart swelling with gratitude. "I will."

With those heartfelt words, Tom gave his son a final pat on the back before stepping aside, allowing Luke to take his position at the front of the aisle. The soft melody of a string quartet began to play, signaling the start of the ceremony.

***

The town square was transformed into a picturesque setting, adorned with the elegant décor from Founder's Day. Twinkling lights hung from the trees, and floral arrangements added bursts of color to the arches and pathways. Guests gathered, their faces glowing with happiness and anticipation.

The music swelled as the groomsmen, Tommy and Gabe, formed a line beside Luke, their smiles bright and supportive. The bridesmaids, Sadie and Hannah, began their graceful walk down the aisle, their dresses flowing as they made their way to their positions.

Emma appeared beneath the arch, the gown shimmering in the sunlight. Her eyes met Luke's, and in that instant, everything else faded away. The world seemed to stand still as their gazes locked, a silent affirmation of their love and commitment.

Emma took a deep breath, soaking in the moment—the square, her friends, her family, and the town that had become her home. Her heart swelled with emotion as she began her walk toward Luke, each step bringing her closer to the man she loved.

As she reached the end of the aisle, her father stood ready to officiate the ceremony, his voice warm and proud. "I trust you with my girl, Luke. So, let's get the two of you married, finally!"

Laughter rippled through the crowd, breaking the tension and filling the air with joy. The vows were exchanged with heartfelt sincerity.

"Wherever you go, I will go," Emma whispered, her voice steady and full of emotion.

Luke's eyes shone as he repeated the words. "Wherever you go, I will go."

Daniel smiled, his heart full as he delivered the final words that would bind them together. "I now pronounce you husband and wife. What God has joined together, let no one separate."

Without hesitation, Luke pulled Emma into a deep, loving kiss. The crowd erupted into applause, the gossips letting out satisfied sighs as if they had known all along how this day would end.

As they walked down the aisle hand in hand, Luke leaned in to whisper, "I love you."

Emma squeezed his hand, her heart overflowing. "I love you, too."

***

As dusk turned to evening, the lights strung around the square began to twinkle against the backdrop of the deepening sky. The crowd buzzed with excitement, eager for the celebration to continue. The band finished playing the first song, and Daniel, Mary, and Tom stepped up onto the small stage, grinning from ear to ear.

Daniel took the microphone, his voice filled with pride. "Ladies and gentlemen, please welcome the newlyweds—Luke and Emma Hunter!"

The crowd erupted into applause, the sound carrying across the square. Emma blushed at the sound of her new name, and Luke beamed as he held her hand, leading her onto the dance floor. The band began to play "Can I Have This Dance For The Rest of My Life," the romantic melody filling the night air.

Luke pulled Emma close, spinning her out onto the dance floor with an easy grace. Their eyes met, and the world around them seemed to melt away. As the music played, they moved together, their first dance as husband and wife full of tenderness and love. The lights above them twinkled like stars, and the soft murmurs of the crowd faded into the background as they shared this intimate moment.

When the song ended, the guests clapped and cheered, their hearts full of joy for the happy couple. Luke dipped Emma with a playful grin, and she laughed, her cheeks flushed with happiness. Together, they made their way back to the stage where their friends and family eagerly awaited the next part of the evening.

Meanwhile, Sadie and Linda had been hard at work coordinating the cutting and serving of the cake. Sadie, ever the perfectionist, made sure everything was in order, while Linda moved around the table with ease, her new role as event coordinator shining through.

"All set?" Sadie asked, giving Linda a quick nod.

"Ready," Linda replied with a smile.

The cake was cut, and slices were passed around to the waiting guests, who quickly dug into Sadie's famous sweet rolls—now transformed into the wedding cake centerpiece. The flavors were a hit, and the dessert table quickly became the center of attention.

With everyone enjoying their cake, it was time for the bouquet toss. The ladies lined up in the center of the square, excitement buzzing in the air. Sadie, Hannah, Linda, and a couple of the town's most notorious gossips joined the group, their eyes fixed on Emma as she prepared to throw the bouquet.

"Ready, ladies?" Emma called out with a teasing smile.

The women exchanged glances, readying themselves for the toss. Emma turned her back to the crowd, holding the bouquet in her hands. She spun around playfully and tossed the bouquet high into the air. Time seemed to slow as the flowers flew toward the group, every eye tracking its descent.

To everyone's surprise, the bouquet landed directly in Sadie's arms. For a moment, she stared at it in shock before quickly tossing it over to Linda, who caught it with a delighted squeal.

Linda's eyes lit up, her face flushed with excitement. "Oh my goodness!" she exclaimed, hugging the bouquet tightly.

The crowd erupted into laughter and applause, the playful moment bringing smiles all around. Sadie winked at Linda, and the gossips exchanged knowing glances, their whispers filling the air as they commented on the unexpected bouquet toss.

"Well, that was... perfect," Hannah teased, nudging Sadie with a grin.

Emma laughed, shaking her head. "I guess the flowers knew where they were meant to go."

As the evening continued, the atmosphere in the square remained one of joy and celebration. Friends and family danced, laughed, and enjoyed the warmth of the summer night, united in their love for the newlyweds and the special moment they all shared together.

***

The evening had been filled with laughter, dancing, and celebration as friends and family gathered in the square to honor Luke and Emma's love. The sky had fully darkened, but the twinkling lights strung through the trees and around the square kept the atmosphere warm and magical.

Luke and Emma had just finished mingling with their guests when Luke gently took Emma's hand, leading her away from the noise of the reception to a quieter corner near the edge of the square. The sounds of the celebration still drifted through the air, but here, it was just the two of them, bathed in the soft glow of the lights.

Luke turned to her, his eyes sparkling with happiness. "Well, Mrs. Hunter, are you ready to get on with our life together?" he asked, his voice filled with excitement and love.

Emma smiled up at him, her heart swelling at the thought of their future. "I've been ready for this moment for a long time," she replied softly, squeezing his hand.

Luke grinned, leaning in closer. "Well, I've got a little surprise for you. I've reserved a cabin in the mountains for the next two weeks. It's all set up, waiting for us. Are you ready for our honeymoon, honey?"

Emma's eyes widened with delight. "A cabin in the mountains? That sounds perfect, Luke! I can't wait."

They shared a quiet, intimate moment, their future stretching out before them, filled with love and endless possibilities. Luke kissed her softly on the forehead, and they both knew this was the start of something truly beautiful.

Just as they were about to rejoin the party, the crowd caught sight of them, and a ripple of excitement spread through the guests. Someone had handed out small favor bags of birdseed, and soon everyone was gathered around, preparing for the grand send-off.

As Emma and Luke walked toward the exit, their hands intertwined, the guests began tossing handfuls of birdseed into the air, showering the couple in well-wishes and laughter.

"Here's to a lifetime of happiness!" someone called out.

The seeds fluttered down, and Emma laughed, shielding her face as Luke pulled her close to protect her. They made their way through the joyful crowd, smiling and laughing as birdseed rained down over them, a playful, lighthearted end to a perfect evening.

Hand in hand, they left the square, ready to begin their honeymoon and their life together as husband and wife.

Chapter Twenty-Three
Getting on With Forever!

THE MORNING SUN STREAMED through the windows as Emma and Luke stepped out of their car, the crisp mountain air filling their lungs. Their cabin in the mountains had been everything they dreamed of and more—a serene retreat surrounded by towering trees, a gentle creek nearby, and the promise of peaceful days ahead. The two weeks of their honeymoon had been a perfect escape, a time to celebrate their love and begin their journey as husband and wife.

As they entered their new home, Emma's eyes sparkled with delight. The cabin was cozy yet spacious, with rustic wooden beams and large windows that framed the breathtaking landscape outside. Luke took her hand, guiding her through each room, his heart swelling with pride and happiness.

"This place is perfect, Luke," Emma said, her voice filled with awe as she ran her fingers along the smooth countertop in the kitchen. "I can't believe it's ours."

Luke smiled, his eyes meeting hers with unwavering love. "I knew we'd love it here. It's everything we ever wanted."

After unpacking a few essentials, Emma decided to prepare some iced tea for the two of them. She moved gracefully around the kitchen, her hands deftly working as she filled a pitcher with fresh tea leaves and slices of lemon. The familiar rhythm of their teamwork felt comforting, a testament to the life they were building together.

Meanwhile, Luke glanced out the window, catching sight of the front porch adorned with a charming swing—a perfect spot for quiet mornings and starlit evenings. He knew this would be the perfect spot for quiet moments together.

A few moments later, Emma heard the soft creak of the cabin door opening. She looked up, surprised to see Luke standing there, a gentle smile on his face.

"Come join me," he called softly. "Let's have our tea on the front porch."

Emma, still holding the pitcher, felt a flutter of excitement. "Alright," she replied, carrying the tea towards the front door. As she stepped outside with a tray of glasses, she spotted the swing and smiled, realizing Luke had done it just for them.

The swing was gently swaying in the breeze, inviting them to sit and relax. Emma set the tray down on a small table nearby and turned to Luke, her eyes wide with surprise and delight.

"You did all this?" she asked, her voice tinged with awe.

Luke nodded, his gaze tender. "I wanted our first moments back home to be special. This swing... I thought it would be perfect for us to settle in."

They settled into the swing, the motion gentle and soothing. Luke poured the iced tea, handing a glass to Emma before taking one for himself. The sun was beginning to set, casting a warm, golden glow over the trees and the front of their home.

"You know," Luke began, his voice soft, "when we were teenagers, we walked by this house and talked about living here someday. I always imagined this day, but I never knew exactly how it would unfold."

Emma lifted her head, meeting his gaze. "I remember those walks. We had so many dreams and plans."

Luke nodded, squeezing her hand gently. "I wanted to make those dreams a reality. Not just the house, but our life together."

Emma smiled, her heart full. "I can't wait to spend the rest of my life with you, Luke."

As they settled into the swing, Emma reached into her apron pocket, her hand closing around something small. "I have a surprise, too," she said, her voice light with excitement. She pulled out a pregnancy test stick, holding it up for Luke to see.

Luke's eyes widened in surprise, his heart skipping a beat. "Emma... is that—?"

Emma nodded, her smile growing wider. "I picked up a few of these tests at the convenience store on the way home. And they all agree—we're going to be parents!"

Luke's expression shifted from shock to pure joy. He pulled her into his arms, spinning her gently on the porch swing. "Emma, this is incredible!"

Tears of happiness welled up in Emma's eyes as she hugged him tightly. "I can't believe it. We're going to have a family."

They sat together, holding each other close, their hearts brimming with excitement for the future. The news of becoming parents added another layer of love to their already perfect day.

***

Deciding that this moment was too special to keep to themselves, Emma and Luke called their closest friends and family to share the wonderful news. Sadie, Hannah, Tommy, Gabe, Mary, Daniel, Tom—and to everyone's surprise—Jenkins and Linda—arrived at their home, their faces lighting up as Emma and Luke announced they were expecting.

"Congratulations, you two!" Sadie exclaimed, pulling Emma into a warm embrace.

Tommy grinned, clapping Luke on the back. "Looks like the Hunter family is growing, huh?"

Mary smiled warmly at Emma. "You're going to be wonderful parents. And, we're going to have so much fun decorating a nursery here!"

As everyone settled into conversation, the mood was light and celebratory, but eventually, the topic turned to recent events—the arrest of Kevin, the involvement of the FBI, and Jenkins' decision to testify.

Jenkins cleared his throat, addressing the group. "I've been thinking a lot since everything went down with Kevin, and I'm looking forward to testifying against him, hopefully he'll go away for along time," he began. "I made mistakes, big ones. And the way I was wrapped up in it all... I still can't believe how I get a chance to start over again."

"Well, what matters is you did the right thing in the end," Daniel said, nodding encouragingly. "And you helped bring Kevin down. That was no small feat."

Gabe leaned in, curious. "What happened with Kevin's investors, anyway?"

Tom filled in the group. "The investors pulled out as soon as they realized Kevin was going down. He's facing charges for fraud, bribery, and who knows what else. They want no part of his mess, but it will be a while before they get their money back, since it's evidence of some of the crimes."

Emma added, "It's a relief, really. The town is safe, and Kevin's plans to manipulate the town are over."

Jenkins sighed, the weight of his involvement still heavy. "Now that it's all behind me, I've been thinking about what I can do next—for the town. I owe a lot to this community."

Tom rubbed his chin thoughtfully. "What Carter's Creek could use is some new business opportunities. We're a small town, but we could really benefit from someone investing in local businesses. You were always good with projects, Jenkins. What if you helped develop something for the community?"

Jenkins nodded slowly, the idea taking root. "You know, I've been thinking about that. A business incubator, maybe? A place where new ideas can grow. We could bring in small businesses, help them get started here. It'd create jobs and keep our town thriving."

Daniel smiled, nodding in approval. "That sounds like a solid plan. It could benefit a lot of people, and it'd give you a chance to rebuild your standing in the community."

Jenkins smiled, hope returning to his eyes. "I like that. It's time to give back to the town in a way that makes a real difference."

Sadie chimed in with a wink. "And maybe you can keep an eye on us small businesses while you're at it. I'm sure Sadie's Bakery could use some expert advice now and then."

Linda, who had been bustling around as the newly appointed event coordinator, stepped into the conversation, her presence now fully integrated into the family dynamic. "Jenkins, I think your idea is fantastic. I'd love to help coordinate the events and promotions for the incubator. We can leverage the community's strengths to make it a success."

Jenkins turned to Linda, gratitude evident in his eyes. "Thank you, Linda. Your support means a lot."

Mary nodded in agreement. "Absolutely. We all want to see Carter's Creek thrive, and this sounds like a great step forward."

Emma smiled, feeling the unity of her friends and family. "It's wonderful to see everyone coming together to support each other. This town is truly special."

As the conversation continued, the group discussed logistics and potential ideas for Jenkins' new venture, the atmosphere filled with optimism and a renewed sense of community spirit.

***

With the excitement of their new home and the news of their impending parenthood, Emma and Luke felt more connected than ever. They spent the evening planning and dreaming about their future, the porch swing serving as a symbol of their journey—a place where they could pause, reflect, and cherish each other.

As the stars began to twinkle above, Emma leaned into Luke, her heart full of love and hope. "I can't wait to start this new chapter with you."

Luke kissed the top of her head, his voice filled with promise. "Me neither, Emma. This is just the beginning of our forever."

They sat together on the porch swing, hand in hand, ready to face whatever life had in store for them, knowing that their love would guide them through every joy and challenge.

About the Author

Meet Judy Best, the island-living, dream-chasing, queen of her home!

For several decades, Judy has lovingly nurtured her family, raising two amazing kids, and now cherishes every moment as she spoils her two granddaughters with beach days and tropical adventures. A few years ago, she and her husband swapped the mainland hustle for the serene sands of Puerto Rico, creating a life filled with sunshine, adventure, and the closeness of a family that thrives together. And after 45 years of love and partnership, their story is still unfolding with as much excitement and heart as the day it began.

A love for reading was instilled in her by her mother, who took her and her two brothers to the library every week. Judy checked out the maximum number of books allowed, reading them all before it was time for their next weekly visit. As a child, Judy boldly declared, "I'm going to write books when I grow up!" And guess what? After all these years, she started writing books!

She began writing non-fiction self development books, because she knew the impact these books would have to change and better lives of others. Her first book was **Mastering Small Talk**, kicked off her *Mastering Life Series*, her second book was **Mastering Friendship**, Book 3 is all about **Mastering Personal Growth,** and Book 4 was**, Mastering Parenting Adult Kids** — continuing her journey to make not only her own dreams come true but to help others find their way to a lifestyle of continuous personal growth. Each of the books in this series can be read on their own, but if you enjoy one, you'll probably enjoy the others, too!

After successfully kicking off that non-fiction series, Judy turned to a genre she enjoys, romance novels, but wanted to write a good love story that could stand on it's own without the need for steamy sex scenes. That's exactly what's she's done with her first two books of the *Carter's Creek Love Story* series, **Love in Small Places**, and **Love's Hidden Treasures**.

Ready to reach for more? Judy's got you covered. Swing by **Judy Best.com** to dive deeper, grab a free companion workbook, and get the support you need to crush your goals. Judy is also available for coaching calls. Please follow Judy Best on Amazon, sign up for her newsletter at www.JudyBest.com to stay abreast of what's happening with the Best family!

Made in the USA
Columbia, SC
14 November 2024